Jane Goodwin Austin

Moonfolk

A True Account of the Home of the Fairy Tales

Jane Goodwin Austin

Moonfolk
A True Account of the Home of the Fairy Tales

ISBN/EAN: 9783744767842

Printed in Europe, USA, Canada, Australia, Japan

Cover: Foto ©Andreas Hilbeck / pixelio.de

More available books at **www.hansebooks.com**

MOONFOLK.

MOON-FOLK

BY

JANE G. AUSTIN

ENGRAVED BY

W. J. LINTON

W. SWAN SONNENSCHEIN & CO.
LONDON.

MOONFOLK.

A TRUE ACCOUNT

OF

THE HOME OF THE FAIRY TALES

BY

JANE G. AUSTIN.

ILLUSTRATED BY W. J. LINTON.

LONDON :

W. SWAN SONNENSCHEIN & CO.,

PATERNOSTER ROW.

1882.

Butler & Tanner,
The Selwood Printing Works,
Frome, and London.

TO

ROSE STANDISH AUSTIN.

Do you remember, my little Rose!
  The twilight hour not long ago,
When, leaning upon my knee, you said.
  In thoughtful accents, soft and slow :

" The *truly* stories, I think, mamma,
  Are not as nice as the Fairy Tales—
Couldn't we go to where such things are,
  In a magic ship with enchanted sails ! "

Long after you lay asleep that night,
   I thought of your wistful question, dear,
Wishing with you that these fancies bright
   Might be true somewhere, if not just here

And I wondered if I might build that ship,
   With its magic helm and enchanted sails,
And if you and I might make the trip
   To the wonderful Land of the Fairy Tales.

The ship is builded, my little Rose !
   We cannot set sail an hour too soon,
For childhood's dreams will change to those
   That never come true, though we reach the moon

J. G. A.

CONTENTS.

CHAPTER I.

THE CHIMNEY-ELF.

RHODA sat in the cupola at the top of the house, reading a book of fairy tales; the Chimney-Elf, who had been for a long time amusing himself by turning somersets upon the narrow cornice surrounding the top of the chimney, had at last grown tired, and seated himself cross-legged beside the kitchen-flue, up which a thin stream of blue smoke was lazily curling.

It was late in the afternoon, and the clouds, which all day had been wandering about the sky as if they did

not know what to do with themselves, had within the
last hour drifted rapidly toward the west, and taken the
shape of a wonderful palace of gold and crimson and
deep purple, with pillars and doorways, and arches and
domes, and spires, such as never were seen out of cloud-
land—a palace for the sun; and he, tired with his day's
work, was rapidly sinking toward it, when Rhoda, looking up from her book with a little sigh, fixed her eyes
upon the clouds, and said, dreamily:

"Aladdin's palace wasn't as splendid as that, I know,
even if he could have had the roc's egg. I should like
to see it, though. Oh, dear, I wish fairy stories were
true!"

"Why, they are, child! Didn't you know that?"
asked the Chimney-Elf, a little contemptuously.

"No. I mean really and truly true! just like going
to school, and to meeting, and your dinner, and your new
shoes," said Rhoda, glancing at her own new shoes.

"Well, they are as true as all those things, if you
only go to them, instead of sitting there and wishing."

"Go to them, Chimney-Elf! why, how can anybody go to a story?" asked Rhoda, opening her eyes
wide.

"Of course you can go to 'hem. Fairy stories and
all that sort of thing live in the moon, and you've only
to go to the moon to find them," replied the Chimney-
Elf, moving a little farther into the smoke.

"Fairy stories live in the moon?" repeated Rhoda.

"Yes, my dear. But that's a very bad way you have of echoing a person's words; very rude, indeed; and I've told you so before."

"I know it, but—how do they live there?"

"How! How do you live in Yankee-land?"

"Why, I—just live here."

"And they—just live there; and when the moon shines they come sliding down the beams, and get into people's heads, and they write them down and call them their own, and that's the way fairy stories, and poetry, and all that, comes into the world."

"Oh, but, Chimney-Elf, if I should go to the moon, could I see all these beautiful stories going on, just as people do all round here?"

"Yes."

"What! see Cinderella, and Little Red Riding-Hood, and Beauty and the Beast, and Jack the Giant-Killer, and all the rest of them?"

"Yes, yes, yes!"

"And Robinson Crusoe, and the Arabian Nights, and Jack and the Beanstalk, and—"

"Every thing and every body, I tell you! Every story that ever was written is true somewhere or somehow; men and women are not bright enough to make anything up; all they can do is to tell over what they have seen and heard. Well, some things are true of the world just about you, and those you call real; and some other things you don't see are just as true, and those you call unreal ; and all the unreal true stories come from the moon, and are real stories there."

"Oh, Chimney-Elf, I wish I could go to the moon ! " exclaimed Rhoda, catching her breath.

' Well, why not ? "

" Why not go to the moon ? "

" Yes."

" Because I can't get there."

" Oh, yes, you can, if I tell you how."

" Can ! Oh, do tell me how, dear, good Chimney-Elf."

" There, none of that. I don't like coaxing, and I am no dearer or gooder than if I didn't know how to go to the moon."

" But—will you tell me how ? "

" Perhaps I will. You can only go once a month, and, as it happens, to-night is the very night for this month."

" Why only once a month ? "

" Because the moonglade only comes right once a month."

Rhoda knew the moonglade, for she lived upon the sea-shore ; she had often watched the broad, shining track of light, which, at a certain point of the full moon's upward course, seems to lead straight across the sea, from the earth to the sky, if only one knew how to pass over it ; sometimes, also, the rising or setting sun produces a sunglade, like a river of molten gold, or rather of pure fire, flowing across the ocean toward the earth ; but few eyes can bear the awful splendor of this sight, and few hearts are so brave as to wish to tread that fiery path and explore the fierce wonders of the sun. The moonglade is very different, and a great many people, not altogether children, have longed to make a bridge of it Rhoda had often wished so, and when the Chimney-Elf suggested the idea, she seized upon it at once:

"Oh, can we go up the moonglade?" cried she; and the Chimney-Elf, puckering his queer little face into a hard knot, winking his bright little eyes very fast, and nodding his head until the cock's-feather in his pointed hat waved wildly to and fro, replied:

"Yes, we can go up the moonglade, if you will behave like a sensible child, and not be frightened. All that you have to do is to come down to the beach a few minutes before sunset, for you know the full moon rises just as the sun sets, get into the dory, and paddle a little way out from the shore. I will be there, and do all the rest. You must not tell a mortal creature where you are going. I don't want everybody rushing to the moon, and making it common."

"Nobody will care what I do," said Rhoda, a little sadly. "Father is going to marry the Widow Merriam, and he goes to see her every night as soon as we have done tea; and my sister Susy is so busy getting the house ready for father's wedding and her own, that she don't remember me when she don't see me; and Mrs. Marsh, who helps her, only says:

" ' Massy me! if that child was mine, I bet she wouldn't be wasting her time and eyesight over books that way!' And Susy laughs and says:

" ' It's all the fun she wants, poor little Rhoda!' So I go on reading; and father and brother Ben always bring me a book when they go to the city with marketing."

" There, that will do, you chatterbox," interrupted the Chimney-Elf, who had rather a crisp temper. " Do you suppose I have lived in this chimney ever since it was a chimney, for something over a hundred years before you were born, without knowing all about the family. And isn't it just because you *are* lonesome and neglected, and given to books and dreams, and nonsense generally, that I have taken notice of you? Try to tell *me* what goes on under this roof—do ! "

And with a scornful toss of the head in the pointed hat, the Chimney-Elf turned a double somerset upon the edge of the chimney, and with the last turn disappeared down its black throat.

" I'll be in the dory at sunset, Chimney-Elf ! " called Rhoda after him, in rather an anxious voice; for she had discovered that her smoky friend was very uncertain in his temper, and sometimes became so vexed at the merest trifle that he would not speak or show himself for months at a time. He did not now deign a reply to Rhoda's words.

It was with considerable doubt that the little girl

slipped out of the house, as soon as tea was over, and made her way to the wharf of loose stones at the foot of the hill, where her father's boats lay—some at anchor, some hauled up on the beach, and one, the dory, made fast to a great post set in the end of the wharf. Few girls of Rhoda's age—she was just past her twelfth birth-day, did I say?—would like to venture themselves alone in any sort of a boat; but she had been brought up by the sea, and could not remember the time when it seemed strange to her to sail or row, or swim or wade, upon or through the water. Of late she had learned to handle the oars for herself, both strongly and well; seeing this, Ben had made a pair of light paddles expressly for her use, and the dory was always left so that she could get it when she wanted—much as some other little girls have a pony-carriage or a veloci-pede, or perhaps a rocking-horse under their own con-trol.

So when Rhoda, in leaving the house, said to her sister:

"I'm going out in the dory a little while," Susy only replied:

"Go along, but don't stay out after dark," and then almost forget that there was such a child as Rhoda in the world.

"If I should stay up in the moon, I wonder if they would miss me down here?" thought the little girl, stopping at the top of the hill to look back at the house

1

and at the figure of Jonas Morton coming up the path to the door, meeting her father, who was setting out for Mrs. Merriam's. Then Rhoda, walking on rather soberly, tried to remember how her mother looked, and wondered whether she should know her if she should meet her in the moon, or anywhere.

She was still wondering, as she slipped the loop of the dory-line over the top of the great post, and stepped into the little boat just as the sun disappeared in the cloud-palace she had watched building for him. Using one of the paddles, she pushed the dory away from the wharf, and then seating herself upon the middle thwart, she left the boat to drift gently up the ebbing tide. Leaning her chin in her two hands, and her elbows upon her knees, she fixed her eyes upon the gorgeous west, and began again to wonder about her mother and herself, and the sun and the moon, and so many other things, that she could not have named them all if she had tried.

In fact, Rhoda found a great deal in the world to wonder at; and as she seldom talked about her thoughts, the wonders were not explained, but still remained wonders, waiting until the time when Rhoda should be grown up; for then, of course, she would know everything, like other grown-up people.

"Well, my dear, do you intend to go on dreaming all night in that mooning fashion?" asked the Chimney-Elf's shrill voice. "Although, why I should call it mooning I don't know, since you have your back to the moon. Turn round, and see where we are!"

Rhoda roused herself with a little start, and saw the Chimney-Elf seated astride the tiller, steering the boat by the pressure of one foot or the other upon the bench below.

"Why, where did you come from, Chimney-Elf?" cried Rhoda, who never could get used to her little friend's odd ways and rapid movements.

"Never mind me, child. Turn round, and look!" said the Chimney-Elf.

Rhoda, changing her position, uttered a little cry of surprise, for the dory seemed to be gliding swiftly along a shining river of light, with a wall of darkness at either side, and at the end a great world of splendor, an immense globe, blazing with light as vivid as it was soft and soothing.

"Can that be the moon, the same old moon that shines into the kitchen windows, and that Bruno barks at?" asked Rhoda; and then, without waiting for the Chimney-Elf's reply, she moved softly forward to the bows of the boat, and sitting upon the little deck, with her feet hanging over almost into the water, fixed her great eyes upon the wonder before her, and fell into a dream more delicious than any she had ever known before, sleeping or waking.

The Chimney-Elf, watching her, twisted his queer

face into its queerest smile, and balancing himself cross-
legged upon the tiller, pushed the pointed hat back from
his forehead, and fixed his eyes upon the moon; while
the little boat, unurged by sail or oar, flew along the
shining track toward its shining goal.

CHAPTER II.

THE MAN IN THE MOON.

"NOW, then!" said the Chimney-Elf; and Rhoda, starting, rubbed her eyes and stared about her. The bows of the dory had struck with a low grating sound upon a beach of glittering golden sand; and the Chimney-Elf, making a flying leap from the boat to the shore, stood politely holding out his hand to help his companion; but as he was only a little taller than Rhoda's knees, his help was not so valuable as it might have been.

"What shall we do with the dory?" asked the little girl, as she reached the beach.

"Oh, it will take care of itself, and wait for us as long as we like. The dory knows," replied the Chimney-Elf, nodding his head until the cock's-feather danced again in the soft light that filled the place, making everything as clear as in the noonday of the earth; yet touching all with a tender, dreamy beauty, such as moonlight lends to even the commonest objects.

"Oh, how I like to be here!" said Rhoda, with a little sigh of delight.

"Wait until you see some of the people; then you may not like it so well," said the Chimney-Elf. "Suppose we should meet the wolf that ate up Red Riding-Hood, or some of the giants that Jack didn't kill: they all live here."

"I don't believe they will hurt me," said Rhoda bravely, but at the same time looking all about her.

"Oh, Chimney-Elf!" cried she suddenly, "I forgot to ask you. Do the people out of the stories keep on doing those same stories over and over, or do they do new ones all the time?"

"Well, it is very much in the moon as it is in the world," replied the Chimney-Elf. "Some people like to do the same things over and over, and think that because they always did them, they are the best things possible to do, and that all the rest of the world ought to do so too: others like a change. But we will call upon the Man in the Moon, who can tell you everything about the people here, even better than I can, though I came from here in the first place."

"You did?" asked Rhoda in surprise.

"Yes. But here you are—that's the house." The Chimney-Elf pointed to a large house, a little way back from the beach, a house remarkable principally for a very high cupola on the top, and a large thorn-bush planted directly in front of the door. Beside this thorn-bush sat a pleasant-looking man, with a lantern between his feet and a dog lying beside it. In one hand he held a large lump of green cheese, from which he took an occasional nibble. All the time, he was watching and laughing at another man, who sat cross-legged upon the ground beside him, with a large bowl of milk-porridge upon his knees, which he was trying to eat; but as it was frozen hard, his only way of doing so was to split off little bits with his pocket-knife, and eat them off the point of it.

"There's that idiot, the Man from the South, again," snarled the Chimney-Elf in a low voice. Before Rhoda could ask who the Man from the South might be, the Man in the Moon turned round for another nibble of his cheese, and seeing them, cried out:

"Why, here's the Chimney-Elf, and Rhoda along with him. How d'ye do, Rhoda?"

"Very well, I thank you, sir," replied Rhoda, wondering how the Man in the Moon came to be so well acquainted with her; and, as the wonder passed through her mind, he said:

"Why, it's because I so often send you fancies and dreams by the moonbeams. I never went down myself but once, and that was all a mistake. It was when Diana got lost, you know, Chimney-Elf."

"Yes. Tell Rhoda about that," said the Chimney-Elf, seating himself upon the ground, and pulling his pipe out of his hat-band.

"Well, I will," replied the Man in the Moon, delighted at finding a new listener for his old story.

"You see, Rhoda, my daughter Diana — by the way, I have several more girls, Cynthia, Luna, Phœbe, and one or two more whose names I have forgotten; but Diana was the favorite. She was always rather a tomboy, liking to play with bow and arrows, and run races and romp with the dogs, better than to read, or sew, or put the house in order. At last she took to going down to the earth almost every night; and the people who saw her were so pleased with her, that they built temples for her to live in, and gave her flowers and jewels, and flattered and praised her until the girl's head was fairly turned. She played all sorts of wild tricks upon her admirers. Why, there was a young man named Actæon, who offended her in some way, and she turned him into a stag, and set his own dogs to chase him; they chased him right out of the world, and up here to the moon: they have not caught him yet, that I have heard of. After that, Diana fell in love with a young man called Endymion, and declared she would marry him. When I heard that, I thought it was high time to go and bring her home. So I told one of the moonbeams to inquire where she was last heard of. The moonbeam, it seems, asked a saucy boy, who, not knowing what she meant, put his finger on his nose and said:

"She's gone to Norridge, of course."

The poor little moonbeam took it all seriously, and brought back that report to me. So I slipped down on the next moonglade, and went all about asking my way to Norridge, getting laughed at for my pains; for it seems that in those days "Gone to Norridge" meant the same that gone to Jericho, or Noddler's Island, or Dixie, or any such expression means now: there was no place in the world really called Norridge. So I came home again, and sent my dog down next, and a half-a-dozen moonbeams with him. The dog was to find Diana, and the moonbeams to tell her that if she would come home, and bring Endymion, I would set them up at house-keeping, and all should be forgiven. So she came; and they live just over the hill near the Cheese Mine."

"But there is a place called Norridge pretty near where I live, when I am at home; only they spell it Norwich," said Rhoda timidly.

"Oh, yes; after my inquiries had made the name so popular, a good many towns were called Norridge," replied the Man in the Moon. "Only, you see, I came down too soon, before they were built."

"Oh, dear! oh, my! o---h!" groaned the Man

from the South, dropping the knife into the bowl of porridge, and clapping both hands over his mouth.

"What's the matter? Burnt it again?" asked the Man in the Moon, staring at him.

"Y---e---s; oh, dear me! oh, my! oh, dear!"

"That's rather curious, Rhoda, isn't it?" said the Man in the Moon, turning to her. "This Man from the South, you see, has a trick of blowing hot and blowing cold in the same breath; and so long as he remembers to blow cold on his porridge it does very well, for he considers ice quite a luxury; but sometimes he forgets and blows hot, and that heats the frozen porridge so suddenly that he burns his own mouth. Silly enough, isn't it? But it's the way he always did do, and I suppose it is the way he always will do."

At this moment there was a terrible crash in the thorn-bush close behind Rhoda. Turning suddenly round, she saw a man scrambling his way out of it, with his face all torn and bleeding, and holding both hands tight over his eyes.

"There's another idiot!" exclaimed the Man in the Moon. "And one who thinks himself wondrous wise too. Come, turn round, and run with might and main, old gentleman."

" Which way, which way? Oh, my eyes, my eyes!" screamed the man, dancing about first on one foot and then on the other.

"Straight forward as you are now; one, two, three—and away you go—run!"

So the man who was so wondrous wise, still holding his hands over his eyes, ran straight forward as hard as he could, until he tumbled into another thorn-bush growing near by: after floundering round in it for a few moments, he broke through upon the other side, and walked away in a very dignified manner, calling over his shoulder:

"Eyes! who says I haven't eyes! I fancy I can see as far into a millstone as most men, at any rate."

" I've read about him, and the Man in the South, and —and you too, sir," exclaimed Rhoda suddenly; "all in Mother Goose: that is just what the Chimney-Elf said!"

" What—that the stories people down there call fairy-stories, and Mother Goose, in fact—stories, are all true up here? Yes, that is correct, quite correct," said the Man in the Moon, stooping to pat his dog, and looking up sideways at Rhoda. "All fancies, and a great many ideas, come from the moon. The moonbeams go when people are asleep, and put them into their heads, and when they wake up they write them down, and call them their own."

"Everybody don't write them down," suggested Rhoda.

"Everybody don't get them!" replied the Man in the Moon. "The moonbeams know whom to carry them to. Sometimes, however, they make a mistake, and stuff too many fancies into the brain of somebody who can't write them, or tell them, and so get rid of them, and he keeps them stored away until they turn his brains upside-down. Then the other people, who never were troubled with fancies or ideas, call these poor stuffed people lunatics—thinking that my daughter Luna has made them what they are, I suppose; and they shut them up in lunatic asylums. Lunatics, indeed! If they only had gone to a writing-school when they were young, they would have been called geniuses, and nothing could have been too good for them. Sometimes the moonbeams pour in ideas faster than the brain can arrange or put them together, even if the person does write them down, and then they make queer work enough of it for a while, but finally join the lunatics. But the Chimney-Elf is growing cross, and you and he had better go on: see what you can, while you stay! I'd take her to the Cheese Mine, Chimney-Elf."

"Well, if you ever stop talking, I mean to," snarled the Chimney-Elf, who had been fidgeting for a long while, but the Man in the Moon only laughed at his ill-temper.

"Right over Old Woman's Hill," said he, pointing.

As the Chimney-Elf and Rhoda walked away they heard the Man from the South cry out:

"Oh! oh! oh! oh! I've burnt my mouth—oh, my mouth!"

Rhoda was going to say something pitiful, and the Chimney-Elf was just beginning to scold, when both of them were stopped by such a chorus of yells and screams and shrieks, all in childish tones, that Rhoda stood still, looking as if she would begin to cry herself.

"What's the matter?"

"That noise? Oh, it's only the Old Woman that lives in the Shoe putting her babies to bed. They cry that way just for fun, you know: she only pretends to whip them; she's as good-natured as she can be. Here's where she lives, just at the foot of the hill."

And turning a corner in the road, Rhoda found herself close beside a monstrous shoe, with a ladder leaning against its side. Upon the ground close by stood a great kettle with a little broth in the bottom, and about fifty iron spoons lay scattered around.

"They eat right out of the kettle," explained the Chimney-Elf. "Poor thing, she has so many children she don't know what to do; and as for baking bread enough for such a family, it is quite out of the question, so they never have any. Run up and look into the shoe, if you like."

So Rhoda ran up the ladder, and peeping over the edge of the shoe, saw a stout red-faced woman, with a switch in her hand, either whipping or pretending to whip a small boy, whose cries may have been playful, but certainly were not pleasant. All at once the woman seized the little fellow by the shoulders, and tilting him over, laid him at the end of a row of children lying close together, and reaching out of sight into the depths of the shoe.

"There, you're all done for now, and I will go and help toss Sister Broomster," said the old woman.

Rhoda crept swiftly down the ladder—the old woman following, saying to the Chimney-Elf:

"You see, my family is as troublesome as ever, Mr. Chimney-Elf; but they are all quiet at last, and I am going out for a little recreation."

"Going to toss Mother Broomster, eh? Nice recreation that, for those who like it," said the Chimney-Elf. "Well, Rhoda, we may as well see the show. Come along."

CHAPTER III.

OLD WOMAN'S HILL.

HURRYING along, Rhoda and the Chimney-Elf presently came to a door leading directly into the hill they had begun to climb, and found the Old Woman who lives in the Shoe knocking upon it and calling out:

"Come, sister, come along; we are late already!"

"Yes, yes, I'm coming, coming right along," replied a cracked voice; and the door opened to let out another old woman, who, when she saw Rhoda, bobbed a funny little courtesy at her, and said:

"How d'ye do, Rhoda! I'm the Old Woman that lives under the Hill; and if I don't move, I suppose I shall live there still. Come along, Sister Shoester!"

So the two old women, with Rhoda and the Chimney-Elf following close, climbed up the hill, and about halfway to the top were joined by another old lady, the fussiest, most restless, worrying old lady who ever lived. Under one arm she carried a loaf of bread, and under the other a bottle of cold tea; and when she was not eating she was drinking, and, whether eating or drinking, she never was quiet—no, not for one single minute.

"Oh, how d'ye do, Mother What-do-you-think?" called out the Chimney-Elf as this old lady appeared. "What do you find to agree best with your delicate stomach, now-a-days?"

"Is that you, Chimney-Elf? Well, I do declare! And Rhoda too! How d'ye do, Rhoda? I'm proper glad to see you. First time you ever came to the moon, isn't it? What were you asking, Chimney-Elf—what do I find to live on? Well, I hardly know; but I expect victuals and drink are the chief of my diet, just as they are of most folkses; and—oh, my! I do declare, if there isn't Sister Banbury on her White Horse, and all her jewelry. I never did!"

"There, that's enough, What-d'ye-think," interrupted the Chimney-Elf; and then turning to Rhoda, he showed her a large wooden cross set up on a plain, some distance below the hill where they stood. Beside the cross a small boy was holding an old white horse, and two more were helping an old lady to step up into a chair, and from that to seat herself upon the horse's back.

"That's Banbury Cross," said the Chimney-Elf, "and Mother Banbury lives just beyond it, with her three little boys: the one holding the horse is the Baker's Man.

who spends most of his time patting the cakes, and marking them with T ; one of the others goes round with a basket to sell hot cross-buns, when his mother happens to make any ; and the other is apprenticed to the blacksmith, who shoes the old horse, and shoes the old mare, and lets the little colt go bare. But it won't do to let it go bare much longer, or he'll have the Society for the Prevention of Cruelty to Animals after him.   Hark ! "

Rhoda listened, and heard the jingling of musical bells, and looked around for a church steeple, but saw none.

" It isn't sleigh-bells, for there isn't any snow," said she.

" Sleigh-bells, pho ! " said the Chimney-Elf. " It's Mother Banbury. Look at her now ! "

And as the old lady rode slowly up the hill upon her white horse, Rhoda perceived that every one of her ten fingers was covered with rings to the very tips, and the

ends of her boots were cut off to let out her ten toes, to every one of which was tied a little silver bell, all of different sizes ; and as she rode, Mother Banbury rang these bells by the motion of her toes, and produced the most charming music you can imagine—that is, from such a source. Besides all these, Mother Banbury wore a chain of large glass beads wound ten times round her neck, which hung all over

2*

the front of her dress; and she wore bracelets and ear-rings, and a large hoop in her nose; and a great bunch of hair on the top of her head, stuck full of feathers and flowers, and jewels, and bows of ribbon, with long floating ends; and she had a great silk balloon tied round her waist, which stood out behind; and a stiff lace ruffle round her neck; and a droll little hat pitched over her eyes: altogether she was a very curious-looking person.

" Mother Banbury is fond of dress," quietly remarked the Chimney-Elf; " and so is Margery Daw. See her ? "

Looking where he pointed, Rhoda saw a queerly dressed young woman among the bushes beside the road, following Mother Banbury up the hill, but keep-ing out of sight as well as she could. She was dressed in rags and tatters to be sure; but she had managed to put them on so as to imitate Mother Banbury in the most laughable manner. Even her ornaments, which were all made of straw, were braided into bands and tied into rings, and split into feathers—in fact, arranged in every possible style to imitate jewelry and ornaments. As for the bells upon her toes, she had made them of nut-shells, with a few little pebbles in each to make the music.

Rhoda wondered whether Mother Banbary would know, if she could see it, that Margery Daw's dress was so close an imitation of her own. But before she could ask the question of the Chimney-Elf, the Old Woman who lived in the Shoe cried out:

"Oh, here's Sister Broomster. Now let's toss her!"

Rhoda turned to look, and saw an old woman coming up the hill with a broom over her shoulder, and a blanket tightly rolled up under the other arm. She was a very clean, nice-looking old woman, with her hair combed smoothly back, and a handkerchief tied over her head; her dress turned up in front, and pinned behind; and her sleeves rolled tightly up to her shoulders. As she came to the top of the hill she threw down the blanket, and, turning her broom upside-down. leaned upon the handle of it while she took breath Then nodding to the other old women, they seized upon the blanket and spread it carefully upon the ground.

"How d'ye do, Mother Broomster?" said the Chimney-Elf, who had a word for every one. "Haven't you got the sky clean yet? You have been at it ever since I can remember."

"Well, no, Chimney-Elf," replied Mother Broomster turning her head sideways and looking attentively at the sky. "There are a few cobwebs left—those white things, don't you see?"

"Why, those are clouds!" interrupted Rhoda.

All the old women stopped spreading the blanket, and looked severely at her.

"Little girl," said the Old Woman who lived in the

Shoe, "did you ever try to teach your grandmother to suck eggs?"

"No, ma'am," replied Rhoda, remembering the switch she had seen in the shoe.

"Then, don't you ever do it, my dear," said Mother Broomster good-humoredly. "As for those being clouds, isn't it likely that I should know what they are, better than you, when I have been all my life sweeping them down for cobwebs, and you never went near them?"

Rhoda did not venture any reply to this question. The blanket being now spread, the old woman tucked her sleeves a little higher, felt of the handkerchief upon her head, grasped the broom in both hands, and laid herself down upon the blanket.

"Now then," said the Old Woman who lived in the Shoe, seizing one corner of the blanket; the Old Woman who lived under the Hill took another, Mother What-d'ye-think the third, and Mother Banbury the fourth; while Margery Daw behind the bushes spread her shawl upon the ground, and pretended to do all that Mother Banbury really did.

"Now, then!" cried all the old women together; and raising the blanket from the ground, they began shaking it, at first with a gentle, regular motion, then harder and harder and harder, until with one great shake they sent Mother Broomster flying out of it away up toward the stars.

"She's going seventy times as high as the moon,"

said the Chimney-Elf. "It's lucky she don't have to start from the earth, isn't it? But, listen!"

"Upward beat, downward beat, inward beat, outward beat. Sing!" said Mother Banbury, waving her sunshade up and down, and in and out, and shaking the bells of first one foot and then the other.

"Sing!" and the four old women, and Margery Daw behind the bushes, threw back their heads, opened their mouths very wide, and sang:

> "Old woman, old woman, oh, whither so high!
> To sweep the cobwebs from the sky,
> And I'll be back again by-and-by."

"Why," exclaimed Rhoda, "they sing the whole of it! I should think they would wait, and let Mother Broomster answer for herself.

"Nonsense, child," replied the Chimney-Elf, with a twist of his comical face; "you don't understand scientific music. The sense has nothing to do with it—the sound is everything."

"But I don't think it sounds as well as if the right one made the answer," insisted Rhoda.

"That's because your musical education has been neglected, my poor little Rhoda. But come, we needn't stay here any longer: they'll keep on singing that until she comes down to-morrow morning. We'll get on toward the Cheese Mine, and on the way look in at the dancing-hall."

So saying, the Chimney-Elf led the way down the other side of the hill. About halfway he turned off into a level nook set round with bushes and paved with large flat stones: at one end of this space sat a cat with some music upon a stand in front of him, and a fiddle beside him. Fixing his eyes upon the music, the cat extended his four paws with all the claws out, and began to scratch and tear at the fiddle-strings with all his might, accompanying his efforts with the most horrible screeches and yells imaginable. The noise was frightful, but at the same time so funny, that a small dog, whose business it was to howl in chorus with the cat, was able to do nothing but roll upon his back from side to side, stuffing his fore-paws into his mouth to stifle the peals of laughter, which would have offended the cat very much if he had perceived them. In the centre of the dancing-ground a red-and-white cow was gravely and laboriously performing a polka in the old-fashioned style of jumping up very high and coming down very hard. The only spectators were a pewter dish and iron spoon, who seemed to be tired of the ball, and were just stealing away among the bushes.

"I suppose you've heard of the Cow that jumped over the Moon?" said the Chimney-Elf. "People generally suppose that she lived on the earth, and jumped up over the moon and down again; but such people could never have noticed a cow's habits very particularly: they never jump high, but, like the one we just saw, they often jump about, over the moon's or the earth's surface. This cow is coming out as a ballet-dancer as soon as Barry O'Lynn can find time to make her a belt with a fringe to it."

"See here, Chimney-Elf. Who are those people knocking at the door of that pretty little cottage," asked Rhoda softly, for the cottage was close beside the road.

"Why, that's Tadpole Frog and the Rat—don't you know? Wait, and I'll make Tad tell you himself. Hallo, Tad! what are you doing there?"

The young gentleman thus addressed turned round, looking very much frightened, and, taking his opera-hat off his head, made a low bow, pulled down his yellow waistcoat, and said:

"Oh, I thought it was ma, you know. I—I'm going to make a little call, Mr. Chimney-Elf, I and the Rat."

"A little call, eh! Why, who lives here?"

"Miss Mouse, I—I believe."

"Miss Mouse! She's a spinster, isn't she?"

"Ye—yes, sir."

"And you're going to 'woo her for your bride,' as the song says?" asked the Chimney-Elf roguishly.

"Ye—yes, sir."

"Well, I suppose your mother is willing, Tad, eh?"

"Mother she—well—I—I can't say, Mr. Chimney-Elf," said Tadpole, looking very much frightened. The door opening just then, he and the Rat rushed in, with more haste than politeness. At the same moment

Rhoda espied a cat and three kittens creeping along toward the Mouse's house, and noticed that all four of them wore mittens.

"They'll take them off before they go in," said the Chimney-Elf, nodding. "They won't handle poor little mousie with mittens, I can tell you; but then she shouldn't have opened the door. That was the trouble."

CHAPTER IV.

THE CHEESE MINE.

RHODA was still wondering why the Mouse should not have opened the door to Tadpole Frog and the Rat, and whether she had perhaps left it open, so that the Cat and her Kittens would get in too, to handle them all without mittens, when the Chimney-Elf said:

"Here we are over the hill, at the Cheese Mine."

"Oh, is this the Cheese Mine?" asked Rhoda, looking down into a great hole beside which the Chimney-Elf had stopped.

"Yes; you know that the moon is made of green cheese—sage-cheese, some wise people call it, because sage means wise, and it is only sage people who know much about the moon, especially the inside of it. Well, the most of the cheese does not lie upon the surface, you know, but has to be dug for, like gold and silver upon the earth. This is the principal mine. Would you like to go down?"

"Very much," replied Rhoda; so the Chimney-Elf took her close to the mouth of the mine; and seated her behind him upon a sled, and told one of several men, who stood looking on, to set them off. The men nodded, and pushing the sled a little way, fitted the runners into two grooves hollowed for them, and gave it a shove. Looking down, Rhoda now perceived that a roadway extended round the inside of the shaft, leading spirally downward like the thread of a screw, and that the sled, once started upon this spiral road, had nothing to do but to spin round and round, and down and down, until it reached the bottom. Breathless and dizzy, Rhoda held tight to the Chimney-Elf, who talked all the time; but not a word of what he said reached her ears, until, as the sled reached the bottom of the shaft, she heard him say:

"And that is the true story of Richard Whittington."

"Oh—Whittington and his Cat!" exclaimed Rhoda. "I am so sorry I did not hear that. Do please tell it to me again, Chimney-Elf! I couldn't listen, coming down the shaft."

"Why, I was saying that after Whittington left London with his cat in his arms, and stopped under the

tree to hear Bow-bells ring out 'Turn again, Whittington, Lord Mayor of London,' he went to sea; but instead
of landing in a savage country, as the story says, he
got shipwrecked, and floated about the ocean on a raft,

he and his cat together, until, while he was fast asleep
one night, his raft got into a moonglade, and when
Richard awoke he was in the moon. He did not know
it, however, and nobody took the pains to tell him. I
doubt if he ever found it out. While wandering about,
soon after his arrival, he came upon the Cheese Mine.
Being rather hungry, he asked if he might go down and
dig his luncheon for himself. The miners told him that
nobody could go into the mine, on account of the rats
and mice who had taken possession of it, and who would
eat a man as quick as they would a candle, if he came
in their way.

"'Pooh!' said Whittington; 'if that is all, I will
send Bow-bells down first, and he will soon clear the
way.' Bow-bells, you understand, was the name of
the cat, given him in honor of the handsome promise

that had recalled Whittington to London. But when the miners understood him, they all cried out, 'No, no! that won't do; for what will the Marquis of Carabas say?'"

"That was the name of Puss in Boots," interrupted Rhoda.

"Yes," replied the Chimney-Elf. "And, as the miners explained to Whittington, Puss in Boots, after he had grown rich and got his title, became very proud and lazy; the more good fortune that befel him, the more he wanted—like some other people. Among the rest of his privileges, he had obtained that of keeping all the rats and mice in the Cheese Mine for his own pleasure and use; so that when he fancied to go hunting, either alone or with his friends, he might always know where to find plenty of game. A very nice arrangement for the Marquis of Carabas, you see; but not so nice for the poor people whose cheese the rats and mice lived upon while waiting for the Marquis to come and kill them. Well, the miners explained all this to Whittington, and to Bow-bells, who stood listening, with his back very much arched, and his upper lip quivering away from his sharp white teeth. When they had heard the whole story, Whittington laughed aloud, and stooping to smooth Bow-bells' rounded back, he said:

"'Why, that's all nonsense. Puss in Boots has no right to keep rats and mice to eat up other people's cheese; and what's more, he shan't do it. Shall he, Bow-bells?'

"Bow-bells gave a *miau* of defiance that sent every

mouse in the mine to his hole for shelter. Then he
went down among them—and such havoc as he made!
All the galleries were choked with the bodies of the
slain, and the whole neighboring country was overrun
with the fugitives who managed to escape. Not a rat,
not a mouse was left to show his tail.

"Bow-bells had finished the battle, and was just sitting down to lick his paws clean, when a message was
brought that the Marquis of Carabas desired the presence of the cat and the man who had invaded his domain,
and meddled with the game sacred to his use.

"Whittington, after consulting Bow-bells, replied
that if the Marquis of Carabas wished to see either cat
or man, he must come to them, as
they were too busy to go to him.
That message brought Puss in
Boots upon the scene very quickly, and a grand fight ensued between him and Bow-bells, Whittington standing by to see fair
play on one side, and Puss in
Boots' former master on the other.

"Bow-bells beat, as might
have been expected, for the Marquis of Carabas had almost forgotten how to fight, and had become very fat and lazy since he
came to his fortune, having no need to hunt, except
for amusement. Bow-bells beat, and the Marquis was

THE MARQUIS.

very glad to come to terms. He agreed henceforth to allow him to kill as many rats and mice as he wanted; to live in the Cheese Mine as long as he chose; in fact, to do exactly as he pleased, so long as he would allow the Marquis of Carabas to creep away home, with ragged ears, and great patches torn out of his sleek velvet coat.

"Bow-bells, having always been poor, and obliged to earn his own living, did not know how to spend his time in indolence, but just kept on with his work until the Cheese Mine was entirely cleared of mice, both living and dead; for the former he drove away, and the latter he devoured.

"For this service, the Man in the Moon presented him with a vote of thanks, and a silver tea-set. To the first, Bow-bells replied, Miau! and as for the second, he suggested that a handsome sum of money given to his master, and a free passage for both of them back to earth, would be much more to the purpose. The Man in the Moon held a council, and concluded to do as he was requested, although quite sure that his own plan was the best. So they gave Whittington a bagful of gold, and sent him back upon the next moonglade to the earth—the moonbeam who conducted him taking the precaution to steal the memory of his visit out of his head while he was asleep, lest he should make the secrets of the moon common and vulgar. The cat remembered it all well enough, but along with the memory of his visit, Whittington lost the power of understanding Bow-bells' language, and even the knowledge that he had a language; so that, although almost any cat you meet could tell you the story of Bow-bells' duel with the Marquis of Carabas, there is not a man, woman, or child on earth who ever heard it, or who knows the true origin of Whittington's fortune. But come, Rhoda, this is not seeing the Cheese Mine."

So saying, the Chimney-Elf got up from the sled, where they had all this while been seated, and briskly led the way down a gallery into the mine at their right. This gallery was lighted by clusters of fire-flies in cages hung upon the walls at regular intervals, and the walls themselves, as well as the ceiling and the floor, were entirely composed of cheese cut as smooth as marble, presenting a beautifully polished and variegated surface —its general hue a delicate green, but streaked and mottled with yellow. Through the middle ran a narrow railway. Soon after the visitors entered it, a low rumbling noise announced that a car was approaching.

"Stand this side with me," said the Chimney-Elf; "and you will see something curious. The work in this mine is almost all done by mites."

"Mites! What are mites?" asked Rhoda.

"Little creatures, first cousins to the spiders, who are so fond of cheese that they can't be kept out of it; and as the air here is unhealthy for men, they prefer to make the mites do the work, who take their pay in cheese."

"But do the mites like it?" asked Rhoda, doubt-fully.

The Chimney-Elf shrugged his shoulders.

"The men are the strongest, my dear," said he; "and the mites ought to be very thankful to have some one take care of them, and give them cheese to eat. Here comes the car. See the little things pull!"

And as he spoke, a tiny car, loaded with one great lump of cheese, made its appearance, looking at first as if it moved of itself; but examining it closely, Rhoda saw that hundreds of little cords were tied to the front and sides of this car, and to the cords were attached millions of mites, who thus pulled it along quite easily.

"You have seen the Performing Fleas, haven't you?" asked the Chimney-Elf.

"No, but Susy has. Jonas Merton took her to see them," began Rhoda, but the Chimney-Elf cut her short.

"They are stronger than the mites, but then there are not so many of them. Besides, the cheese wouldn't agree with them. The mites like it."

"And is all the cheese got in this way?" asked Rhoda, remembering the great lumps she had seen in the Man in the Moon's hand.

"Oh, no. This is the principal mine; but then there is a great deal of cheese found just below the surface, and that the inhabitants can pick up for themselves. In some places, every man has his cheese-cellar in his own

yard, and when he wants a piece, just steps down and
cuts it out of the wall. Now, there's the Little Boy
that lived by himself—I dare say you have heard of
him; he mines his own cheese, and we will step up
and see him. This way."

And striking into a side-cutting, the Chimney-Elf led
the way through a long winding ascent, and finally came
out upon the surface of the moon, close by a neat little
house with a wheel-barrow standing at the front door.
A pretty young woman sat at the window and smiled
at Rhoda, while a brisk-looking young man was just
coming from the back of the house with a hammer and
some nails in his hands.

"Hallo, Little Boy!" shouted the Chimney-Elf.
"Going to mend that wheel-barrow again?"

"Why, yes," replied the man, stopping and looking
thoughtfully at the wheel-barrow. "But the old thing
never will stay mended since that first time."

"What time? Tell Rhoda about it," broke in the
Chimney-Elf. And the man, still looking thoughtfully
at the wheel-barrow, slowly said:

"Why, it happened this way, Rhoda. When I was
young, I was quite small, so that they used to call me
Little Boy; and in fact, they do so now. But after
father and mother died, I lived here by myself, and
kept house the best way I knew how. I've got a
cheese-cellar out here, and I made my own bread and
such things. When I had finished a meal, I'd just put

3

the bread and cheese on a shelf in the kitchen; after a while, though, the rats and the mice that Bow-bells sent wandering all over the moon, found me out, and I had no peace day nor night from them. At last, one day, as I was laying about me with a broomstick, trying to kill or drive away a few of my tormentors, Baron Bluebeard, who was riding by, stopped to see what was the matter; for I suppose I made a good deal of noise. When I had explained the case to him, he smiled horribly, and said:

"'Get a wife, Little Boy, that's the way to do. Get a wife!'

"Then he rode on, and I sat down to think of his advice. It seemed to me pretty good; and the next time I went to Moonopolis, I asked Lydia Locket to marry me. She agreed, in case she found her pocket before the wedding. While we were still talking, Kitty Fisher stepped in to say that she had found it. The only trouble then was, that the Lockets lived in the very middle of the city, and the lanes were so narrow that no coach could get into them, although some of the streets were ridiculously wide. The only way seemed to be for me to bring my wife home in a wheel-barrow; for of course the Lockets, who are very smart people, would not let a daughter of theirs walk to her wedding

"Lydia agreed to the wheel-barrow, and we were married all right; but on the way home, the unlucky wheel-barrow broke down, and spilt Lydia into the mud, all dressed in her beautiful pocket, trimmed with green lace, and the rest of her wedding finery."

"Well, I didn't scold, Little Boy, did I?" asked the pretty young woman at the window, laughing merrily; and Little Boy looked up at her and smiled, then down again at the wheel-barrow and sighed.

"No, you didn't scold, Lydia," said he. "But I never have been able to mend the wheel-barrow from that day to this, and I don't believe I ever shall."

"That'll do. Come along, Rhoda, and see the House that Jack built," said the Chimney-Elf, pulling Rhoda by the sleeve. Away they went, leaving the Little Boy that used to live by himself staring dismally at the wheel-barrow, and Lydia Locket laughing out of the window at him.

CHAPTER V.

THE EGG-WOMAN.

"THERE'S another little boy," said the Chimney-Elf, as he and Rhoda came once more into the road. "But I don't think much of him; he's ashamed of the good old mother who brought him up."

"Who is he?" asked Rhoda, gazing about her.

"Cross the road and look into that square pit in the field opposite: you will find him there."

Rhoda did as she was bid, and looking down into the pit, found it about half full of gold-dust, in which a mean-looking man was rolling, and grubbing, and rooting, very much like a pig in a mud-bath. Upon the

farther bank of the pit sat an old woman, very poorly
dressed, looking very neglected, but watching the mo-
tions of the man in the pit with the greatest delight.
As Rhoda approached, she looked up and spoke to her,
as everybody here in the moon did, with no appearance
of surprise, and without waiting for an introduction.

"An' would yer look at him, Miss Rhody? Sure an'
it's himsilf is me own b'y, that twinty years ago, whin
he wor a little b'y, he washed his mommy's dishes; an'
now he is a big b'y, he rolls in goolden riches; an' isn't
that same a glory an' a j'y to the mother that 'nd give
the two eyes out of her head to plaze him?"

"Come, Rhoda!" called the Chimney-Elf; and when
the little girl came back into the road, she found her
friend talking with a shrewd-looking old man, who was
saying, and laughing all the while:

"Yes, asked me how many strawberries grew in the
sea, the great fool! Thought he'd get hold of an old
fisherman, you know, who'd be so flustered with a question like that, he wouldn't find a word of reply to make.
But I guess the fellow got as good as he sent; for what
d'ye think I told him? 'Why,' says I, 'there's as many
strawberries grows in the sea, as there is red herrings
grows in the woods.' He, he, he! not bad, was it, for
an old fellow rising seventy, like me?"

"Not at all bad. I always thought that was a good
story. Come along, Rhoda." And the Chimney-Elf set
off at a great pace, with Rhoda close behind him. "I

want to get out of old Trinculo's way before he tells
that story again," said he. "It is the only good thing
he ever said in his life, and he tells it over and over
and over again."

"Why, Chimney-Elf, look there!" exclaimed Rhoda,
stopping at the top of a little hill they had just climbed,
and pointing down into the hollow below.

"Oh, yes, the Egg-Woman and Stout the Peddler.
That boy's always in mischief! Why, when Johnny Green
threw his father's cat into the well, and Johnny Stout
pulled her out, it was only because he wanted to stone
her. She got away, and went up to London to see the
queen. While she was there, she saw a mouse under the
queen's chair, and pounced upon it in a minute. The
queen was a very nervous woman, and afraid of mice, so
she told Green's cat she would reward her in any way
she chose. Puss asked to be allowed to see the king.
Thereupon the queen had the lord chancellor put it into
his law-books that a cat may look at a king as much as
she pleases, whenever they are in the same room. After
that, one of the great noblemen at the court asked the
cat down to his castle, and confided to her that it was
haunted by a mouse, who every night at fifty-nine minutes past twelve ran up the face of the great clock in
the hall, and, precisely as the clock struck one, ran down
again, making it very unpleasant for the family, if they
happened to wish to look at the clock during that minute.
Pussy Green listened to the story, and then asked time

to consider the matter. The nobleman gave her a
week, and fed her upon cream and chickens every day
At the end of the week, Pussy stated that she could

catch the mouse, and would
do so; but for payment she
was to have a little house
to herself in the noble-
man's park, a servant to
wait upon her, and as
much cream and as many
chickens as she chose to

eat. The nobleman joyfully agreed. Puss hid herself
under the clock, and caught the mouse that very night,
and lives to this day in her cottage in Albion Park."

But of all this long story Rhoda had heard very little,
her attention being absorbed in the scene below. The
Egg-Woman, tired and warm with her long walk, had lain
down beside the road to take a little nap, with her basket
of eggs close beside her, covered by the skirt of her
dress. The lad, whom the Chimney-Elf called Johnny
Stout, and who seemed by the pack upon his shoulders
to be a peddler, finding her lying thus, thought it a good
opportunity to play a practical joke and steal the basket
of eggs; but the old woman's skirts covered it so com-
pletely that he could not get it out. Just as Rhoda
came in sight of them he gave up the attempt, and stood
looking down at the poor, old, tired woman, considering
how he should manage to rob without awakening her.

"I have it," exclaimed he at length; and taking a pair of scissors from his pocket, he quietly cut the skirts all round about, leaving the egg-basket exposed. Then catching it up, he hurried away, turning his head over his shoulder and laughing at the ridiculous sight the poor Egg-Woman now presented. But walking with one's head over one's shoulder is not very safe when one carries a basket of eggs. Johnny Stout had not gone very far before he met Tom, Mr. Piper's son, who had just stolen a pig from Jack's house, and was running away as fast as he could, with Jack after him. Tom was looking back at Jack, and Johnny Stout was looking back at the Egg-Woman. Before either of them knew that the other was near, they ran plump into each other, with such force as to smash every egg in the basket, and to kill the pig, which was half frightened to death already. While the two boys stood staring and gasping at each other, Jack overtook Tom Piper, and seized him by the collar, crying:

"Ha! you young villain, I've got you now, haven't I?" and without waiting to hear Tom's reply, began to lay his cart-whip over the young thief's shoulders in the most liberal fashion.

"Oh, Mr. Jack, please don't any more, please don't!" cried little Rhoda, running down the hill as fast as she could, and beginning to cry herself. At the sound of her voice, Mr. Jack let go of Tom's collar, and he ran roaring down the street toward his father's house, where he found the Piper playing a tune in the cow-shed to his favorite cow, who stood considering whether she had not rather have her dinner.

Mr. Jack meantime turned upon Johnny Stout, who was trying to wipe off some of the egg which ran trickling down his breast, his arms, his legs, and even spattered his face.

"As for you, sir," said the farmer, angrily, "you have been at your old tricks again with the Egg-Woman, have you? Now, I tell you what it is: either you pay her fairly for these broken eggs, and give her a new dress out of your pack, or I will serve you as I just served Tom. Make your choice, and be quick about it."

Johnny Stout looked at the farmer, he looked at the whip, he listened to Tom's roars in the distance, he looked at the old woman, who was beginning to shiver and to freeze from the loss of her skirts, and at last he very slowly began to take the pack off his back, and to pull out a piece of very poor, thin calico.

"I'll give her a dress off that," mumbled he.

"Is that of the same sort as what she has on?" asked Mr. Jack, who was a bachelor.

"Full as good, any way," replied Johnny Stout.

"Why, no, it isn't, you wicked boy!" exclaimed Rhoda. "Her dress is a good thick plaid, and that's nothing but a cheap calico."

"Aha! you know about it, Rhoda, don't you?"

3*

exclaimed Mr. Jack, quite delighted. "Well, here, you look over this fellow's pack, and pick out a dress for her yourself. I've a good mind to thrash him into the bargain."

"No, please don't, sir," said Rhoda, kneeling down beside the pack, and pulling the things over quite as if she enjoyed doing it. There were several pieces of dress-goods, as the shop-keepers call them, and the little girl looked at them all several times, choosing at last a nice thick woollen plaid, a little better than the dress Stout had spoiled. When she had chosen it, Mr. Jack made the peddler cut it off; and then he made him pay two dollars for the ten dozen of broken eggs, the number being neatly written upon a paper pinned upon the handle; and then he let him go, just as the poor old woman started up, exclaiming:

"Why, why, what's all this? Why, sure, this isn't I!"

"Here's a new dress instead of that, and here's the money for the eggs!" cried Rhoda, running toward her with a gift in each hand. But the poor old thing was too much confused to attend to her, and kept looking at her cut skirts and her empty basket, shivering, and shaking, and crying:

"Why, sure, this isn't I! Why, I don't believe Trip would say it was I!"

"But here's a new dress, and "— began Rhoda.

"Lord-ha'-mercy-on-me, I *know* it isn't I!" said the old woman.

" But of course it's you; and here's a new dress," persisted Rhoda.

"Well, if it be I, as I think I cannot be, I've got a little dog at home, and he'll know me," muttered the Egg-Woman.

"Well, here's the dress, and the money, and the basket; but you'd better not put the dress into the basket, because it's all eggy," said Rhoda, rather mournfully, as she put the things into the old woman's hands, and watched her trudge away, still muttering:

"I know it isn't I, but he'll know me."

"I should be pleased to have you and Rhoda come in and rest yourselves in my house," said Mr. Jack, when she had gone. "It's a pretty nice house, as houses go, I think; in fact, I built it myself. A man is apt to be proud of his own work. I've got a good barn, too, and a granary, with some of the prettiest corn you ever saw in your life, stored for winter. The mice troubled me somewhat, and I got a cat to keep them down; but, poor thing, my dog worries the life out of her every chance he gets, and—hillo, what's that?"

By this time the party had come within sight of a fine white house, with a great barn and other buildings behind it. It was toward the yard of this barn that Mr. Jack now pointed indignantly. Rhoda looked, and saw a forlorn-looking young woman, with a pail and stool in one hand, walking toward a cow with one horn curiously crumpled and the other straight, who stood waiting for her. But just as the forlorn young woman set down her stool and pail, a dreadfully ragged man jumped out from behind the barn-door, and running to the young woman, took her round the waist, and kissed her very heartily.

"Well, I declare!" exclaimed Mr. Jack; "if that isn't Bobby Shaftoe got home from sea, and come straight after Dowsabella. Well, I hope she'll cheer up a bit now, for a forlorner creature than she's been, ever since he sailed, you never saw. Why, she'd go round

PRETTY BOBBY.

the house all day long, with the tears running down her face, singing:

> 'Bobby Shaftoe's gone to sea,
> Silver buckles at his knee;
> He'll come home and marry me:
> Pretty Bobby Shaftoe.'

But then nobody thought he ever would come home and marry her, and she grew more and more forlorn every day. The silver buckles seem to have gone, though, and Bobby looks as if the world had treated him pretty badly. Shouldn't wonder but that's the reason he's remembered Dowsabella. Well, well, come into the house, won't you, Chimney-Elf."

But the Chimney-Elf politely declined, and Farmer

Jack, leaving them to go their own road, turned toward the barn-yard, where Dowsabella, Bobby Shaftoe, and the cow with the crumpled horn, stood hugging and kissing, and laughing, and crying, and talking, and mooing all together, and all very happy.

MY LITTLE DOG AT HOME.

CHAPTER VI.

SINDBAD THE SAILOR.

JUST round the corner from Jack's house, Rhoda and the Chimney-Elf met a flock of sheep driven by a pretty girl dressed in a white gown with blue ribbons, a broad-leaved hat trimmed with a wreath of flowers; carrying a crook in her hand, also decorated with ribbons and flowers. She was crying bitterly, and the Chimney-Elf said, as they met:

"Why, Bo-peep, what's the matter? Here's Rhoda come to see you."

"Oh, Chimney-Elf! How do you do, Rhoda? What shall I do? just look at these sheep!"

"What, lost their tails again!"

"Yes, every one; and brother Jack will scold me dreadfully; for it takes so long for them to grow, and he hates to see them that way."

"Bo-peep! Little Boy Blue has been with you, you know he has!" exclaimed the Chimney-Elf severely. Bo-peep hung down her head and twisted the blue ribbons upon her crook.

"Well—just a few minutes," whispered she. "His cows were pasturing along the road as nice as could be, and my sheep were all grazing on the hill, so he and I picked a few flowers, and he made me this wreath. We just talked a little, and then all at once we saw that the cows and the sheep were gone, and we heard his father calling out:

"'Boy Blue! have you gone to sleep under that hay-stack again? If you have'—and then I hunted and hunted after my sheep, and once I sat down to rest, and fell asleep just for a little minute, and when I waked up I was sure I heard them bleating; but I didn't—and then I looked and looked again, and at last I found them; but, oh!"—

And Bo-peep burst out crying again, and pointed to her poor tailless sheep.

"How did it happen?" asked Rhoda tenderly.

"Why, there's an old fox that lives in the wood who, a good many years ago, got his own tail cut off in a trap, and ever since he tries to persuade all the other creatures to cut off their tails. At first he got the other foxes to do so; but now they've grown too wise, and don't do it any more; then he got the monkeys to, but every one laughed at them, so that they all ran away to the earth, and settled a town called Darwin's Holme; and then he came down to the sheep, and they are so silly that they will let him cut off their tails every time he catches them alone, and then he makes soup of them. He's a horrid old thing, and his brother is just as bad: he's the one that stole the old gray goose and the ducks from old Mother Slipper-slopper's barn-yard, and carried them off to his den-O. Didn't you ever hear of that!"

"Yes, I have heard of that. He had some children —one, two, three; and they ate the bones of the goose, didn't they?" asked Rhoda eagerly.

"Yes, I believe so," replied Bo-peep disconsolately. "But I wish they wouldn't eat my sheep's tails too."

"Well, there's no help for it now; so go home, and tell Farmer Jack, get your scolding, and recollect another time not to play with Boy Blue instead of minding your sheep," said the Chimney-Elf, pulling Rhoda by the hand. So the two went on, until Rhoda began to grow tired, and said:

"Chimney-Elf, isn't there some way we could ride to the rest of the places?"

"You're getting tired, are you?" replied the elf, looking up in her face, then nodding a reply to his own question. "Well, yes, there are a good many ways we can ride. There is the famous flying horse that the juggler sold to the Indian prince, which took him to the mountain of adamant and the enchanted palace; but he is an ugly-tempered beast. You know, in the end he switched his tail into the Indian prince's eye, and turned him into a one-eyed Calendar; so we won't have him. Then there's Pegasus; but, poor fellow, he has too much to do already, for they've made a regular hack of him

 for the use of every mortal who can rhyme love and dove, and so call himself a poet. Then there's Don Quixotte's horse Rosinante, but the old Don wouldn't spare him, as he is always on his back himself; and there's Bavieca,

PEGASUS.

and Bayard, and the Hippogriff, and twenty more of whom you never heard. Then there are the Seven-league Boots, what do you think of them? Hop-o'-my-Thumb lives close by, and would be delighted to lend them to you."

"That would be nice; but they might not fit me. And, then, what would you do for yourself?"

"Oh, I can go, like smoke, without any help," said the Chimney-Elf; "and as for fitting, the Seven-league Boots fit everybody, don't you know? The ogre wore them, and then Hop-o'-my-Thumb, and they would suit you just as well. But after all, the prettiest way of travelling I know of, is on the magic carpet."

5

"Oh, I know about that! It is in the Arabian Nights," cried Rhoda, delighted.

"Yes, you remember, Prince Houssain bought it in the city of Bisnagar for thirty purses, and brought it home to his father, the Sultan of the Indies. Then, when his brother Ahmed, by the help of his wife, the fairy Pari-banou, took possession of the kingdom, he found the carpet in the treasury, along with the ivory tube through which you could see anybody you wished; and the apple whose smell cured any sickness, however severe. After Ahmed's death, Prince Ali came to the throne, and being of a prudent turn of mind, he put all his father's and brother's curiosities up at auction, and sold them to the highest bidder. The magic carpet was knocked down to Sindbad the Sailor, who, growing tired of the sea in his old age, and still wishing to travel, found it difficult to suit himself with a conveyance; for, like most sea-faring men, he was a very poor horseman, and very much afraid of a carriage. We might go up to Sindbad's, and see if he will lend us the carpet."

"Oh, do. I should so like to see Sindbad the Sailor!" said Rhoda, clapping her hands.

"Very well. Just the other side of this little wood we shall come upon his country-house. It is rather an odd one, built out of the hulk of an old ship called the Argos, formerly owned by a fellow named Jason, who used it in the wool-trade. Sindbad has fitted it up very prettily, and spends a good deal of time here. In fact, I think it suits him better on the whole than his fine house in Bagdad; it is more in his old original style, you know. That next house, made out of a boat, is where the Peggottys live — old Uncle Dan'l, and Mrs. Gummidge, Little Em'ly, and all. Poor Little Em'ly had rather a hard time of it, but her troubles are all over now, and she is as happy as ever. They take summer boarders too, mostly children. I've seen Little Nell and Paul Dombey, and Tiny Tim, and heaps more of them playing round the old boat, with Little Em'ly standing in the door looking after them, 'most as if she was their mother. There, now, you see Argos Villa!"

The Chimney-Elf pointed, and Rhoda, looking, saw a very curious house, or was it a ship? She could not make up her mind which; for at one end was a beam running out like the bowsprit of a vessel, and where it joined the house, was an image of a golden sheep, like the figure-head of a ship; but instead of masts there were chimneys, and between the chimneys was the week's wash hung out to dry, looking like a full spread of canvas. At the stern were two windows, serving also as doors; in one of them sat a gentleman dressed in loose white trowsers, and a blue shirt, with a turban upon his head, and funny yellow slippers upon his feet. He wore a very long white beard, and was smoking a pipe with a stem at least six feet in length, so that the bowl rested upon the ground at some distance from Sindbad's cushions. A curious little man, about ten inches high, was putting some tobacco into the pipe, which was almost as tall as himself.

"Ah, Chimney-Elf and Rhoda, how do you do? Glad to see you. Take a seat in the smoke, old fellow; I know you like it; and Rhoda, here's a cushion for you.

"Who've you got there?" asked the Chimney-Elf, rudely staring at the little man, and seating himself where the blue smoke of Sindbad's pipe would curl around him.

"That's the King of Liliput, my boy. Picked him up on my eighth voyage," said Sindbad, half-closing his eyes, and peering through the smoke at the little man.

"I thought there were only seven voyages," murmured Rhoda, and was much abashed by the suddenness with which the sailor turned and stared in her face.

"Oh, yes, my dear," said he. "There were a good many more than seven; but after those were written down, I forbid the moonbeams carrying any more of them to earth. I am going to write a book myself, some day, so I am saving the rest of my adventures for that."

"Write a book!" exclaimed the Chimney-Elf contemptuously. "Who says the fools are all dead? You had better go down to earth at once, if you're as far behind the moon's time as that."

"Well, I don't know, Chimney-Elf," repiied Sindbad good-humoredly. "There's a firm of publishers, White Crow, Black Swan & Phœnix, living in Utopia, with whom I have been talking a little. They tell me that about next Millennium will be the time to publish, and I am thinking of going into it. They are to take all the risk, and give me all the profit."

"Ha—yes—I dare say. So you've been to Liliput?" said the Chimney-Elf, staring at the little man.

"Yes, last month. I had grown a little tired of home—Zobeide and Fatima were always quarrelling—so I just sat down on the magic carpet and wished myself where I never had been before. The first I knew, I was sitting in what seemed to be a garden of dwarf plants; but on standing up and looking about me, I perceived that the plants were actually fully-formed trees, and that some little creatures like that fellow were walking about beneath them. I had never heard of such people; but a man who has been around the world as much as I have is not easily taken aback; so I sat down again.

and began to talk to one of them. He was not a bit frightened, but, when I asked him who he took me to be, said, as coolly as possible:

"'One of the outside barbarians from Gulliver Land. We had him here once, and didn't think much of him finally.'

"'Why, you little wretch,' said I, 'I could eat you at one mouthful.'

"'So could a buffalo eat a rat—if he got the chance,' said the saucy little manikin. With that he threw a handful of dust in my eyes, blinding them so that I roared with pain. When I had rubbed them open again, I saw that the whole air was filled with little balloons, most of them of a bright red color, with cars hanging beneath, each car filled with people, who sailed up close to my head, but just so far above it that I could not reach them. From that safe distance they shot tiny darts at my face and eyes, each one stinging like a wasp as it touched me. The worst of all was, that, as every shaft was darted, the whole crowd would roar with laughter, as if I were the most ridiculous object in the world. Indeed, I began to feel myself so. I can tell you, Chimney-Elf, these little folks are pretty formidable enemies, even to a wonderful traveller and a smart fellow like me."

"But how did you get their king to bring home?" asked the Chimney-Elf, nodding.

"Why, there was a little management needed there.

As soon as I could, I made the Liliputians understand that I was a friend, and only wanted to have a little pleasant chat with them—in fact, to ask some advice and instruction of them: there's no way to bring these smart people round like that, Chimney-Elf; and they were taken in directly. They asked me to sit down, and they laid aside their darts, and they brought their king, the court, and all their show folks to see me, and to listen to the talk that was to show how bright they were, and how stupid I was. So I was very polite too, and asked the king to sit upon the carpet beside me. He accepted with much dignity; and the moment I had him there, I wished myself at Argos Villa, and, presto! I was there. Eh, your majesty ?"

The royal captive made no reply, and Sindbad continued : " We're great friends now, though, and it was His Majesty who gave me the idea of writing a book."

" Aha ! " said the Chimney-Elf, " I see it all now."

CHAPTER VII.

ROBINSON CRUSOE.

"PERHAPS you would like to hear an account of my later voyages," said Sindbad, after smoking a little while in silence. The Chimney-Elf made up a face.

"Well, no, I thank you," said he; "I believe we won't trouble you; we are rather in a hurry. We only stopped for a minute, to ask if you will lend us the magic carpet for a few hours."

"The magic carpet? Oh, yes, you can have it for a week, if you like. I do not expect to use it; in fact, I doubt if I ever leave home again," replied Sindbad, settling himself in his cushions.

"So you said between every two voyages," replied the Chimney-Elf scornfully. "Well, where is it?"

"The carpet? Oh, it is in the camphor-chest, to keep it from the moths. Ali!"

Sindbad clapped his hands as he spoke, and a tall negro immediately appeared from the inside of the house-ship: Rhoda recognized him as the slave who was sent to invite Hindbad the porter to eat dinner with Sindbad every day, and pay by listening to his stories.

"Ali, bring the magic carpet!" commanded Sindbad.

Ali, disappearing, returned presently with a small square package under his arm. Untying and unrolling this, it proved to be a small Turkey rug, about six feet square, very dingy in color and considerably worn.

"Is that really the magic carpet?" exclaimed Rhoda, rising and coming closer to it.

"Yes, my dear, it really is. Sit down on it, if you like; but be careful not to wish yourself anywhere; or if you should, take care to wish yourself back here directly," said Sindbad good-humoredly. Rhoda smiled, and timidly seated herself in the middle of the carpet. At the same instant something sprang to her side and caught her by the arm, while a shrill voice cried out:

"I wish myself at home!"

It was the King of Liliput; and before the Chimney-Elf or Sindbad could interfere to stop it, the magic carpet had carried him and Rhoda far above their reach, and the next moment set them down in Liliput. The king immediately jumped off the carpet, and standing at the edge, said to Rhoda:

"I shall not ask you stay and see me, my dear, for what with Gulliver, and what with Sindbad, I have had quite enough of your race, and never desire to see another. I shall let you go safely, although you see the war-balloons are already gathering. But before you go you must promise that you will not return to Sindbad. Of course, he would take the carpet and follow me at once; and although we are quite a match for him, if it comes to war, we are a quiet people and prefer peace. So, unless you promise that you will not give the carpet back to him, I shall have to keep you a prisoner here."

As he spoke, he made a sign with his hand, and from the hundreds of little red balloons floating just over their heads, Rhoda saw thousands of fine cords descending, each cord finished with a little anchor, swinging down toward her.

"They'll catch in your hair, your eyes, your ears, your flesh, and hold you so tight that you will never get away, if once they take hold," said the king; and Rhoda, frightened, cried out:

"I won't go back to Sindbad!"

"That's right," replied the king. "Go, then, where-ever else you like."

"But how shall I find the Chimney-Elf?" asked Rhoda dismally.

"Oh, he will find you. There, you had better go now, my dear. The people do not like to see a Gulliverian." said the king hurriedly; and even as he spoke a cloud of tiny arrows and darts flew from the balloons, wounding Rhoda upon the face, neck, and arms so sharply, that she cried out:

"I wish—I wish I was away!"

Instantly the carpet rose high above Liliput, and the war-balloons; but not having been directed where to go, it remained floating in mid-air, drifting idly with the summer wind, which soon carried it away from the land, and out over the ocean. Rhoda, looking down, felt half delighted, half frightened at her position, and said aloud:

"We're going away out to sea, and perhaps I shall get wrecked upon some desert island. Oh, I wish I could see Robinson Crusoe!"

The words were not of her mouth before the carpet was flying through the air so rapidly as to quite take her breath away: she closed her eyes in terror, but opened them as she felt the slight jar of striking the earth. She found herself landed upon the summit of a high crag, or pile of rocks, and close beside her stood a man dressed in clothes made of goatskin with the hair on, sheltering himself from the sun, under an umbrella of the same material. As Rhoda opened her eyes, this man turned his upon her, and remarked. "Well, I thought I was out of humanity's reach; but it seems I'm not. So that's the last new thing, is it?" continued he, staring at the carpet. "Better than a velocipede, I should imagine."

"Oh! please sir, are you Robinson Crusoe?" asked Rhoda, breathing a little hard after her rapid journey.

"That's my name. I don't keep visiting-cards here."

"I—I've read about you, sir," said Rhoda timidly; for Robinson Crusoe did not seem inclined to make much conversation, nor to be particularly glad to see his visitor.

"Yes, I know one of those meddling moonbeams carried my story, or part of it, down to the earth. I scolded her well for it," said Crusoe, seating himself and taking out his pipe. "You don't mind smoke, I suppose," added he, striking a light with a flint and steel from his pocket.

"No; the Chimney-Elf smokes, and so does father," replied Rhoda.

"Yes—Chimney-Elf? Oh, I know now. Well, is he coming here too? I'm not very partial to visitors."

"I'm sorry I came, then, and I'll go right away," said Rhoda, turning a little red, and feeling somewhat hurt; but Robinson Crusoe laughed, and laid one of his great brown hands upon her arm.

"Don't be in a hurry, little girl," said he. "How did you come here, any way?"

So Rhoda began and told the whole story, from the time of her arrival with the Chimney-Elf at Argos Villa, ending by saying that she had always wanted very much to know more of Robison Crusoe, and begging him to tell her something about himself and his island. At this request Crusoe shook his head.

" You'll go and make a book of it, and that's been done once too often already," said he. " I was vexed enough at that moonbeam for putting it into De Foe's head."

But Rhoda promised so earnestly that she never should think of such a thing as writing a book, and was so eager, and so timid, and so interested, that Robinson Crusoe finally consented to trust her. Settling himself comfortably upon one corner of the carpet, he began his history from the time when he returned to his island, after being rescued and taken home by the captain of the mutinous crew. The rest of the story, as written in the book of his adventures, Crusoe declared to her to be a mistake of the moonbeam's, the truth being that after a short experience upon the mainland, he had found himself so little pleased with the way things were managed, that he had set sail, with his man Friday, determined to return to his island and spend his days there.

After numerous adventures, very wonderful, but not to be narrated without breaking the promise made by Rhoda before listening to them, Crusoe and Friday had found the island, and destroyed the boat which brought them thither, feeling quite sure that they should never wish to leave their retreat again. No sooner was the boat destroyed, however, than Robinson began to long to see his home, and spent all the time not absolutely necessary for catching goats, raising millet, and baking earthenware, in roaming over the island watching for a distant sail. At length, he and Friday with great labor succeeded in building a large canoe, and embarked in it, with a dog, a cat, and a parrot: after nearly starving to death, they reached the shore of an island inhabited only by cannibals, who were on the point of devouring them, when an immense roc swept down, seized them both in her talons, and carried them to her nest. This, greatly to Crusoe's surprise, proved to be one of those built upon the edge of the Valley of Diamonds men tioned by Sindbad; and as soon as he could escape from the roc's nest, he set about finding some means for help-ing himself to a few of the precious stones. This was finally managed by Friday, who, killing a sheep that happened to wander that way, skinned it, and rolled him-self up in the skin. Crusoe then tied him into a compact ball, and rolled him down the cliffs into the valley, where Friday untied himself, and collected a bagful of fine dia-monds. Then remembering Sindbad's account of his own escape from the valley, Friday tied the skin about him and laid down upon his face for a while, until the roc, seeing what was expected of her, flew down and brought him up, getting the carcass of the sheep for her pains.

After that, Crusoe and Friday wandered away into another part of the country, sold their diamonds, and lost the money by trusting it to a man who had always been honest until so fine an opportunity to become dishonest brought out his real character; and finally embarked for home in a ship which wrecked them upon the shores of their own island. After this they remained contented for a while, and then became as anxious as ever to escape: this they finally managed by taming a

pair of whales, and driving them across the ocean in double harness attached to a raft. "But the restless disposition with which I was born," said Robinson, finishing his story, "never will let me remain quiet, in one place or an other. Twenty-seven times, Friday and I have escaped from this island, and twenty-seven times have returned to it. Now I consider myself settled for life; I am disgusted with the world, and never desire to return to it. But, Rhoda, that carpet is a very convenient piece of furniture, is it not? Only to wish, and you are somewhere else! Suppose you get off, and let me try it."

"Don't you do it, Rhoda," said a voice close behind her; and Rhoda, starting round, found the Chimney-Elf seated cross-legged, smoking his pipe as coolly as if he lived in Robinson Crusoe's cave, and had only stepped out for a breath of evening air.

"No, my dear Crusoe," continued he, nodding the cock's-feather wildly forward, "we know you too well: you and Friday had better go to work and build another boat, or tame some more whales, we can't spare you our carpet."

"Oh, well, never mind; I dare say I can make one by thinking it over a little," said Robinson Crusoe carelessly. "Won't you look round, before you go, and see a few of my curiosities here on the island?"

"Rhoda may, if she likes; I think I'll stay by the carpet. And you may as well tell your man Friday to keep farther off. I see his black head sneaking up over the edge of the cliff, plain enough; but you won't get the carpet, Robin, my boy; neither you nor Friday."

"Robin, Robin!" screamed a harsh voice from the cave beneath their feet, at this moment.

"Robin, pretty boy, come see Polly. Robin, Robin!"

"Come and see Polly, won't you, Rhoda?" asked Robinson Crusoe, a little confused at being found out in his plan for letting Friday steal the carpet while he led away the Chimney-Elf; and without waiting for a reply, he led the way down into the cave, followed rather timidly by Rhoda. Upon a perch just inside the entrance sat a pale-green parrot with a yellow head, who, at sight of Robinson, began to run up and down her perch, fluttering her wings and screaming harshly, by way of showing her delight at his presence.

"Pretty Robin, pretty boy! Polly fond of Robin! Polly fond of pretty boy!" cried she; and then opening her mouth and showing her black tongue, she shrieked out a dreadful laugh.

"Isn't she a beauty, Rhoda? Scratch her head a little and get acquainted," said Robinson, fondling his pet.

"Won't she bite?" asked Rhoda, timidly stretching out her hand.

"She! No, indeed; she's as harmless as an unfledged dove," replied Robinson; and at the same moment the parrot darted forward her head and snapped at Rhoda's fingers so viciously that she turned and ran out of the cave as hard as she could, and throwing herself down upon the carpet, cried angrily:

"I wish we were a thousand miles from here."

CHAPTER VIII.

BEAUTY AND THE BEAST.

"WELL, where is this!" exclaimed the Chimney Elf, as the carpet sank rapidly to the ground. "A thousand miles from Crusoe's Island, you said; but where does that bring us? What made you in such a hurry, Rhoda?"

So Rhoda, still very red and angry, told her story, and showed her finger just grazed by the parrot's sharp beak.

"Yes, she's a spiteful creature, and not to be trusted. But where in the world, or where in the moon are we?" asked the Chimney-Elf, shading his eyes with his hand and looking about him. At this moment a little girl tripped out of the wood close beside them, swinging a basket in her hand and singing merrily.

"I know now, there's Red Riding-Hood," exclaimed the Chimney-Elf; and as the little girl came up, he continued:

"How about the wolf, my dear? Has he met you this morning?"

"Oh, no, sir, thank you," replied Red Riding-Hood; "I haven't seen anything like a wolf."

"What, haven't you spoken to any one since you left home?"

"Nobody but a sheep, sir."

"A sheep, eh?"

"Yes, sir; such a nice sheep, all curly and clean as he could be. He said he'd just been bathing in the brook up here."

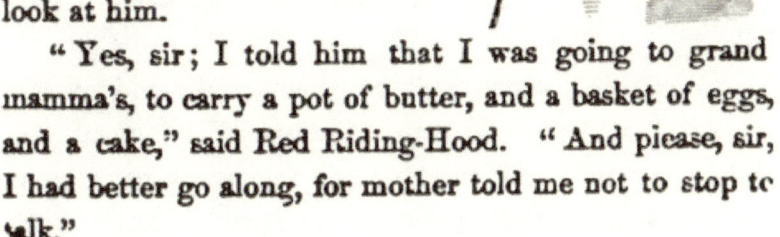

"And did you tell the nice curly sheep where you were going, my dear?" asked the Chimney-Elf, grinning from ear to ear, so that Rhoda hated to look at him.

"Yes, sir; I told him that I was going to grandmamma's, to carry a pot of butter, and a basket of eggs, and a cake," said Red Riding-Hood. "And please, sir, I had better go along, for mother told me not to stop to talk."

"Except with sheep," suggested the Chimney-Elf. "Where is the brook you told about?"

"Just behind those trees, sir. Good bye; I must be going."

"Good bye—you little goose," said the Chimney-Elf. "Rhoda, pick up the carpet, and come with me to look after this brook."

"Why do you want to see the brook, Chimney-Elf?"

"Come along, and don't ask questions. There, I told you so."

He had not told her anything, but Rhoda knew better than to say so, and silently looked where the Chimney-Elf pointed.

"You see that the brook comes out from under that great rock, don't you? And you see the foot-prints of a wolf close to the spring. Then look along down here, ever so far below, and you see the hoof-prints of a sheep. Now search this thicket, and see if you don't find his carcass."

Rhoda peeped into the thicket, and started back in horror, saying:

"Yes, and it hasn't any skin on. It looks dreadfully."

"Well, well, sheep will be sheep to the end of the chapter, I suppose," said the Chimney-Elf mournfully. "The way this wolf supports himself is by coming to the brook, and waiting beside the spring until he sees a sheep drinking lower down. Then he rushes out, says the sheep has muddied the water he was about to drink, and, no matter what the sheep says, he falls upon him and kills him. Sometimes he strips off the skin, washes it clean in the brook, wraps it around his own gray hide, and cheats simple folks into believing him to be a sheep. This is what he has done with Red Riding-Hood this time; and because he wore a sheep's skin, the silly child never suspected that he was the same old wolf from whom she has been rescued so often, and warned against so many times. Come, spread the carpet, and let us go and save her once more."

"Can we—how can we? The wolf will eat us too," cried Rhoda; but still she spread the carpet, and as soon as she and the Chimney-Elf were upon it, he ordered it to Red Riding-Hood's grandmother's cottage, and it was there.

The door stood open, and, without waiting for the Chimney-Elf, Rhoda rushed in. The wolf had already arrived; but the old grandmother, too wise to take a wolf for a sheep, had jumped out of bed as soon as she saw him, and, with the shovel in one hand and the tongs in the other, was defending herself with great courage; while the wolf, with his sheep's skin half slipped off, and his red eyes and white teeth showing underneath the curly white wool, looked more as if he would like to run away than to fight.

"Yah, yah! Get out, you brute!" screamed the

grandmother, waving the shovel wildly in the air, and snapping the tongs within an inch of the wolf's nose.

Her cries were echoed by shrill screams from outside, and the next moment Red Riding-Hood came tumbling into the cottage, frightened nearly out of her senses, and twisting her head nearly over her shoulder to look at a very respectable brown bear who was walking leisurely along the road behind her.

'Oh, grandma! there's a horrid old bear, so big and so ugly, and little bits of eyes and great coarse hair, and such monstrous paws, and he chased me—"

"I am very sorry indeed to have frightened you, my child," began the bear in a melancholy voice, as he crossed the road toward the cottage. "I really did not see you until you began to run and scream and—what sir, are you here, and in your sheep's skin again?"

These last words, of course, were spoken to the wolf, for the bear had now arrived at the cottage door and stood looking in.

"Yes, it's him; and I wish, Mr. Bear, you would give him a lesson that he'll remember. He's forever round this cottage, and my life isn't safe a minute," began the grandmother, who had seen the bear before, and knew that in him she should find a friend. As she spoke, the wolf, now thoroughly frightened, tried to dart out of the door, but was caught by a blow from the bear's paw, which knocked him down and tore away the sheep's skin at one sweep. As he rose the bear met

him with another cuff upon the opposite side of the
head, and then bestowed so sound a drubbing upon him,
that when at last the wolf was suffered to creep away,
he was so ragged, bruised, and miserable a beast that
not even the silliest of sheep need have feared to meet
him. As he sneaked away the bear called after him,
" Remember, this is only a warning! If I catch you at
these tricks again, I will punish you in earnest."

" There, that's what I call justice," remarked the
Chimney-Elf, who had quietly taken a seat upon the
end of the crane in the grandmother's fire-place, and
was refreshing himself with a smoke-bath. " That's
what I call behaving like a gentleman, Mr. Bear."

" Oh, that is nothing. I am not a gentleman, only a
poor, clumsy, ugly beast," said the bear, sighing deeply,
and turning to leave the cottage.

" It is well for some foolish little girls who like to
talk with wolves in sheep's clothing, that there are such
beasts as you at hand," said the Chimney-Elf, scowling
at Red Riding-Hood, who was sobbing in her grandmother's arms.

" Well, I don't know that it is any concern of yours,
Mr. Chimney-Elf," replied the old lady, whose fright
and anger had made her a little cross, but who never
scolded Red Riding-Hood for anything.

" Maybe not, grandma ; but I advise you not to leave
your latch-string hanging out quite so freely when there
are wolves around. Come along, Rhoda."

And the Chimney-Elf made a spring from the end of the crane quite out of the door, and went frisking down the road at such a rate that he and Rhoda soon overtook the bear, who was jogging along in the most melancholy manner possible.

"You live pretty near here, don't you, Bear," asked the Chimney-Elf politely.

"Yes, this is my garden wall," said the bear. "Perhaps Rhoda would like to come in and look at the flowers. I have some very pretty roses, and there's a young lady—"

"Isn't her name Beauty?" asked Rhoda suddenly.

"Yes, my dear, 'Beauty by name, and Beauty by nature.' She's the most charming young lady who ever lived, and you shall see her, if you will," replied the bear, his rugged face quite lighting up with pleasure. Rhoda thanked him, and she and the Chimney-Elf followed through a little gate which he pushed open as he spoke, and found themselves in a large and splendid garden. Roses of every shade bloomed in all directions, and mixed with them were lilies, and pinks, and honeysuckles, and jessamine, so that the garden was as full of perfume as it was of beauty. The humming-birds and honey-bees feasted there all day long, the whirr of their wings mingled with the songs of the birds who crowded the surrounding trees, and the tinkling fall of the fountains that danced and sparkled in the sunshine. It was a lovely garden—so lovely that

Rhoda, stopping a little way within the gate, clasped her hands, and said, only half aloud :

" Oh, I wonder if it isn't the garden of Eden come back. I never saw anything like it, in the world ! "

" And yet she isn't happy here," said the bear, who had overheard the softly spoken words. " Look at her ! "

Rhoda looked and saw a young lady seated beside the principal fountain, throwing flowers into the water. A book lay upon her lap, but she did not seem to care for that or anything else, and looked as miserable and idle as it is possible to imagine.

" That is the way she sits all day," said the poor bear, sighing. " Let us go and speak to her."

But as the young lady heard the steps of the visitors approaching she turned away her head, and sweeping her hand backward with a disdainful air, said :

" There, go away, Beast, go away Isn't it enough to keep me a prisoner here, without tormenting me with your presence ? "

" Oh, Beauty, Beauty, don't be so cruel to me, don't ! " moaned poor Beast, shrinking away as if she had struck him ; and although he hung his head almost down to the ground, Rhoda could see the great tears roll down his hairy cheeks and run trickling down his great nose.

" Poor Beast ! " said she very softly, and turned her back upon the proud Beauty, whom she no longer admired.

The Chimney-Elf looked from one to another with

his shrewdest smile, and finally bounding upon Beast's shaggy head, he whispered in his ear:

"Take Rhoda to the other end of the garden, and give her some of your nicest honey. Be very kind and gentle with her, for she's a timid little thing. I want to talk to Beauty a little while all alone."

So the bear, who was always good-natured and ready to forget his own sorrows when he could help other people, raised his head, and looking kindly at Rhoda, asked her in a very gentle voice if she would walk through the garden with him. Rhoda eagerly answered yes; and as she spoke, Beauty started and looked around.

"Why, who is that?" exclaimed she.

The bear, who was already walking away with Rhoda, did not hear the question; but the Chimney-Elf, who had seated himself upon the edge of the fountain with his feet dangling toward the ground, replied:

"That is Rhoda. Isn't she a pretty girl? The poor bear seems mightily comforted for your ill treatment of him. I think I shall leave Rhoda here altogether."

"I am the mistress of this place, you saucy Chimney-Elf," replied Beauty haughtily.

"The bear is the master, and whoever he chooses will be mistress," replied the Chimney-Elf carelessly. Beauty made no reply, but sat looking uneasily after Rhoda and Beast, who were slowly walking down a path bordered with roses and tulips.

" He seems very happy. I should think it was time he had something to make him happy, poor Beast," continued the Chimney-Elf.

"Where did he pick her up?" asked Beauty suddenly.

" What, Rhoda? We met him at Red Riding-Hood's grandmother's cottage. Do you want to know what he was doing there?"

" I suppose he went to see Red Riding-Hood, or else to meet Rhoda," replied Beauty, tearing up the grass near her, and flinging it into the fountain.

" No such thing. He went there to do good, which is the only pleasure you have left him in life," replied the Chimney-Elf severely ; and then he went on to tell the story of their morning adventure, closing with such a lecture to Beauty upon her pride, and selfishness, and injustice to the poor Beast, who was, he declared, a world too good for her. It ended in her bursting into tears, and calling piteously to the Beast to come and protect her, and tell this odious Chimney-Elf that she was not the horrid, cross, ungrateful wretch he made her out to be.

CHAPTER IX.

THE KNAVE OF HEARTS.

AS the bear, with flaming eyes and furious gestures, rushed to the protection of his weeping Beauty, the Chimney-Elf, skipping nimbly past him, ran to Rhoda, and snatching the carpet from under her arm, jumped upon it and pulled her after him, exclaiming at the same time, "I wish we were in the palace of Aladdin."

Rhoda closed her eyes in terror, for the Beast was almost upon them, and the Chimney-Elf would not have half filled the wide red mouth opened to snap him up; but he did not seem in the least frightened himself, and as the carpet rose, called out mockingly:

" You are the most ungrateful Beast alive! Beauty never cared so much for you as she does at this minute; and if you go back and tell her what a charming girl Rhoda is, she will love you almost as well as you do her."

"Oh, Chimney-Elf, how can you talk so!" exclaimed Rhoda reproachfully.

" Because you are a goose, my dear," replied the Chimney-Elf; and at the same moment the carpet settled to the ground. Rhoda opened her eyes, and found herself in the court-yard of a splendid palace filled with servants and horses and carriages, running this way and that in the greatest confusion.

"The Princess Badroulboudour is going out for a drive," remarked the Chimney-Elf. "After she is out of the way we will go in and look at the palace."

While he was speaking, two or three women-servants appeared upon the steps of the palace, and among them a tall lady dressed with the utmost magnificence, her clothes sparkling with jewels, and stiff with gold embroideries. Her face was covered by a thin veil, but through it Rhoda could perceive that the princess looked very cross and dissatisfied, and had, moreover, lost most of her wonderful beauty. Her voice, as she ordered her servants to place her in the carriage, was harsh, fretful, and impatient, and Rhoda could see that the women made grimaces at each other when their mistress's back was turned.

"She does not look very happy for a princess," said Rhoda, as the carriages jolted and creaked out of the court-yard; for in that country it is not the fashion to put springs under carriages, or to oil the axles of the wheels.

"No," replied the Chimney-Elf, leading the way into the palace; "neither she nor Aladdin are very happy. She never got over her disappointment about the roc's egg, and is in the habit to this day of declaring that her palace is a miserable failure, and the hall of the twenty-four windows no better than a great lantern; all for want of that unfortunate egg.

"Couldn't they find something else as pretty to hang up, instead of a roc's egg?" asked Rhoda.

"Bless you, child, what a goose you are! It isn't the beauty, or the usefulness, or the anything about a roc's egg that makes the princess want it; but it is just the one thing that she can't have; and although she knows that the Genius of the Lamp threatened to eat Aladdin up

alive if he mentioned it again, she is forever urging him to ask for it. Poor Aladdin! Come up and see him."

So saying, the Chimney-Elf, who seemed to know the way around every one's house as thoroughly as he knew their private histories, led the way up stairs and through several magnificent chambers to a little dressing-room, hardly more than a closet, at the very farthest corner of the palace. The doorway was closed by a curtain;

and drawing it a little aside, the Chimney-Elf motioned Rhoda to look in. She did so, and saw a little old man, with rather a mean and cunning but a very unhappy face, sitting cross-legged in the middle of the floor, and stitching away at a pair of wide trowsers.

As he stitched he hummed a dismal tune, and every now and then varied it with a sigh or a groan. All at once the sound of trumpets and horses' feet was heard below, and Aladdin, jumping nimbly up, ran to look out of the window of his hiding-place. In a moment he returned, and sinking down in his favorite attitude, took up the trowsers, muttering:

"My high-born princess is going to visit the Sultan, her father, is she? Won't they just claw and scratch poor Aladdin behind his back? If it were not for Aladdin's money, though, I wonder how my royal father-in-law could pay his quarterly bills, or how my lady princess would buy her new dress for every day in the year. Ho-hum!"

And then he began again upon the dismal tune, and the Chimney-Elf quietly drew Rhoda back from the curtained doorway, and led her through the splendid palace. In the great hall of the twenty-four windows they stopped, and seated themselves to rest upon a divan heaped with cushions of cloth of gold.

"Pretty fine house, isn't it, Rhoda?" asked the Chimney-Elf, stretching his droll little legs and arms, and opening his nut-cracker jaws in a prodigious yawn.

"Yes," replied Rhoda sadly. "But it don't seem to be of much use to anybody. Aladdin hides away in the closet to amuse himself by making trowsers; and the Princess Badroulboudour scolds about him to her father, and don't care for anything because she can't have the roc's egg."

"And never a chimney in the whole house; nothing but those horrid charcoal pots, even in the kitchen. Come!"

And jumping up, the Chimney-Elf threw open one of the twenty-four windows all set round with precious stones and fine goldsmith's work, and led the way out upon a sort of balcony formed of the roof of the lower story of the palace. Here he spread the carpet, and seating himself and Rhoda upon it, said:

"Now where? Who do you want to see next?"

"I should like to see somebody that has everything he wants, and is as happy as he can be," said Rhoda.

The Chimney-Elf laughed, and bid her close her eyes. She did so, felt the carpet rise from the terrace, and a moment later felt it settle down again.

"Look!" said the Chimney-Elf.

Rhoda opened her eyes, and smiled. She found herself seated upon the floor in a neat little sanded kitchen. Door and windows stood wide open, and the afternoon air, laden with summer smells and sounds, filled the whole place. Just opposite to Rhoda, tucked up in a corner so closely that he could hardly move his arms, sat a fat little boy with a great mince-pie in a plate upon his knees, and a piece in each hand. He was so busy with these that he did not notice the arrival of visitors until the Chimney-Elf quietly said:

"Well, you're pretty happy, aren't you, Jacky!"

Jacky did not at once reply. He had lifted the crust of the pie and was eagerly peering under it: presently he thrust in his thumb and forefinger, and dragging out a large raisin, held it up to the admiration of his guests, while he exclaimed in a husky voice:

"See what a good boy am I!"

"You'll be nothing but pie, and before you know it, if you go on at that rate," said the Chimney-Elf.

At this moment, a nice-looking servant-maid bustled into the kitchen and began to make up the fire, saying at the same time, "Well, I do declare, Master Jacky, you're at that pie again. What do you suppose your ma will say?"

For his sole reply, Master Jacky jerked his thumb toward the window. Looking that way, Rhoda saw a merry-faced young farmer leaning with elbows upon the sill, and looking roguishly in. As soon as the nice-looking servant-maid saw him she turned toward the fire and began to blow it vigorously, as if she had not a moment to spare for anything else. The young man at

7

the window laughed a little, sighed a little, and then began to sing:

"Oh, cruel, cruel Polly Hopkins, to treat me so, to treat me so!"

Without looking round, the maid replied, by singing:

'Oh, cruel, cruel Tommy Tompkins, to plague me so, to plague me so!"

"Does it plague you really, Polly?" asked Tommy; and before Polly could reply, Jacky gravely remarked, with his mouth full of pie, "There's ma coming!"

Then making a tremendous gulp, he swallowed what was in his mouth, and crammed in all the rest of the pie, just as an inner door opened, and a brisk, middle-aged woman came into the kitchen, looked all round, and said:

"Why, how do you do, Chimney-Elf? I haven't seen you since you came to my wedding with Harry Cum Parry. Ah, dear! It was in the fruit season, you remember, and what a feast of apples and pears we did have! Since then, you know, I've married again, and now I'm Mrs. Horner. And how do you do, Rhoda? I'm ever so glad to see you. And Tommy Tompkins *as* usual! Well, Polly, put the kettle on, and we'll all have tea. I do declare if there isn't father coming, too? Why, father, what's the matter?"

As Mrs. Horner thus cried out, Rhoda turned to see whom she addressed, and beheld a short stout little man, with bandy legs and crooked toes and a bleeding nose.

In his two hands he carried a large tray filled with deli-cious tarts; and he was running and puffing, and look-ing over his shoulder, with every sign of haste and fear.

"Why, father!" exclaimed Mrs. Horner, setting the cottage door wide open, and motioning Rhoda to stand out of the way.

"Take 'em, take 'em—she made 'em!" panted the little man, thrusting the tray into his wife's hands and running wildly round the room, until coming to a large knot-hole in the partition, he thrust the top of his head into it, and was trying to squeeze himself through, when more hasty footsteps were heard running down the road. In a minute a very angry gentleman, with a red face and beard and fiery blue eyes, darted in at the cottage door, and stood glaring about him, but failed to see Mr. Hor-ner, because Mrs. Horner, with a little scream of terror, had run and put herself in front of him as soon as ever she heard the steps of his pursuer.

"Well, where is that knave?" panted the angry gentleman.

"What knave, pray?" asked Mrs. Horner angrily.

"My knave, madam. The knave of the King of Hearts. I am the King of Hearts, and John Horner, my knave, has stolen my tarts, and with them run away. He ran into this cottage, madam, and I want him—him and the tarts! Give me my tarts! Give me the Knave of Hearts!"

And with these words the King of Hearts, who seemed to be the very most hot-tempered king imaginable, began raving about the cottage, slashing at everything with the sword he held in one hand, or the darts which filled the other.

"Thieves! fire! murder!" screamed Mrs. Horner. "There are your nasty tarts upon the table! Take them and be gone! A fine king you are, to be sure; and if John Horner ever goes back to be your knave, I'll—"

"No, you won't, wife! Don't say it, for I'm going back this very minute, if his majesty will let me," whimpered the Knave of Hearts, creeping out from behind his wife's petticoats, and falling upon his knees at the feet of the king, who was counting the tarts, and looking at one that seemed to have been broken.

"Oh, your majesty, if you would only be so kind as to forgive me, and let my wages go on, I'll be so good," mumbled the knave, while his wife cried angrily:

"John Horner, I'm ashamed of you! wages, indeed!"

"Hold your tongue, wife! Oh, your majesty, couldn't you find it in your royal heart to forgive me?"

"Eh, what's that? Forgive you, did you say? Well, but how came you to touch the tarts, made by the queen herself, with her own royal hands and all! And you stole them!"

"Please your majesty, it was my wife made me do it."

"Made you do it! How's that, Mrs. Horner—what does he mean!"

" Your majesty may well say mean, for mean as dirt it is to have a man tucking off the blame on to a woman that way; though it is no more than Adam did before him, to be sure."

" Well, but why does he say it was you made him steal the tarts!"

" Well, I'll tell your majesty the whole truth. Horner there, has always been telling' me about the queen's tarts, and how nice they were, and how nobody but your majesty could ever taste a bit, and all that, until he made me almost crazy ; for you must know, your majesty, that I make very nice pastry myself—some folks say better than even Bedreddin Hassan who lives round the corner here."

" Bedreddin Hassan, son-in-law of the Sultan of Egypt, husband of the Lady of Beauty, and father of little Agib! Does he live round the corner! Dear me, how very singular!" said the King of Hearts, laying aside his sword and darts, and seating himself upon a corner of the table. "How came he here! I wish I could eat one of his cream-tarts."

" Your majesty shall have one in two minutes," exclaimed the knave, rushing out of the house with all speed.

CHAPTER X.

CINDERELLA.

"HO, ho!" laughed the king. "That's the way he ran when he took my tarts. The head cook saw him and tripped up his heels, so that he fell on his nose; but he was up again and off before the cook could get the tarts. So you wanted to see if the queen's tarts were as good as yours, eh?"

"Yes, your majesty, I did; and I told John to see if he couldn't beg a little piece left on a plate after dinner, or something like that. I never meant that he should steal them, I'm sure."

"No, I dare say not. I'm very fond of pastry," remarked the king.

" Well, now, your majesty, if you would condescend —we were just going to have our tea, me and Jacky, and Mr. Horner, and Tommy Tomkins, and Polly Hopkins, and Rhoda and the Chimney-Elf; and if your majesty would sit down and take a dish o' tea, and taste one of my mince-pies, and a piece of Bedreddin Hassan's cream-tart—"

" And we'll have the queen's tarts too," interrupted the king. " My exercise has given me an appetite, and I should be delighted to get some tea."

" Well now, that's clever!" exclaimed Mrs. Horner. "Polly, is the tea made? Set out the table quick, and let's have it while it's fresh and good."

" But I thought Bedreddin Hassan went home to Egypt with his wife, and her father, and his mother, and Agib," remarked the king, fingering one of the tarts longingly.

" Oh, yes, he did—Polly, the best tea-things—he did, your majesty; but the truth is he'd been a pastry-cook so long, and was so young when he went at it, that he'd rather lost the knack of doing vizier's work, and the Sultan of Egypt felt a good deal discontented with him. Then again, the Lady of Beauty had a good many high notions, and after the novelty had worn off, she used to ask Bedreddin Hassan what was the price of butter to-day, and whether he ever tried pepper on a cream-tart, and questions like that, which didn't make things any pleasanter between them. Little Agib was apt to remember when he first saw his father—and altogether Bedreddin Hassan led a dog's life of it; and one day he just put up a few things in a bundle, and ran away from Cairo and back to Damascus, or rather to this place, which is not far away from Damascus, and opened a shop, where he makes cream-tarts as good as—"

"Here's the knave with a basket full," exclaimed the king, jumping down from the window-seat, and running to the door to meet Mr. Horner, who beamed all over with delight at seeing how well he had come out of his scrape.

"Polly, put the kettle on," said Mrs. Horner, setting one of her own mince-pies, one of Bedreddin Hassan's cream-tarts, and the dish of queen's tarts upon the table, and moving up the chairs.

"Sit down, good folks, sit down," said the king, seizing the first chair he came to, and helping himself to half the cream-tart. Tommy Tomkins, who sat next to Rhoda, gave her one of the queen's tarts, which seemed to her, after all, no better than Susy's Thanksgiving pies; and she was just finishing the last mouthful of it when a horseman stopped before the cottage and called out—

"Any young women in there?"

"Polly, you and Rhoda go out and see if he means

either of you," said Mrs. Horner, pouring out tea. So Polly and Rhoda went, followed by Tommy Tomkins and the Chimney-Elf.

"Can either of you young women put on this shoe?" asked the horseman, pulling a slender glass slipper from his breast, and holding it up in the sunlight.

"Mercy on us! I'm sure I can't," exclaimed Polly Hopkins; but Rhoda, seating herself upon the ground, began to pull off her boot, saying to the Chimney-Elf:

"I know I can't get it on, but I'd like to try."

"Of course you would, being a young woman," replied he. "Why, that's Cinderella's slipper, and nobody but Cinderella can wear it. Her fairy god-mother has taken care of that."

"No, I can't wear it," said Rhoda, hastily returning the slipper to the young man, who rode off with it, while she, as hastily lacing on her own boot, whispered to the Chimney-Elf:

"Let us go and see Cinderella, before the man with the slipper finds her out."

"Very well: spread the carpet!" and in a moment more the two friends had lost sight of Mrs. Horner's cottage, and were softly set down in the corner of a great dark dirty kitchen paved with stone, and dismal to the last degree. At the farther end of this kitchen was a large open fire-place, with a coal fire in one end of it, and a heap of cinders in the other. Upon this pile of

cinders sat a young girl dressed in ragged and dirty old
clothes; her feet bare, and her hair uncombed, her face
unwashed, and her work sadly neglected all about her.
Leaning her chin upon her hand, and fixing her eyes
upon the fire, this untidy young person was saying half
aloud:

"It's too bad, altogether too bad! The prince said I
was the prettiest girl he ever saw, and I know I'm ever
so much better-looking than my sisters, or any other lady
at the ball. It's real mean that I should have to waste
my life here in the kitchen. I was made for something
better than housework, and I think it's too bad."

"Hoity-toity, what's all this!" exclaimed the fairy
godmother, sailing down the chimney, and twisting her
head this way and that, to see if she had got her clothes
dirty in the passage. "Made for something better than
housework, were you, my dear? We'll see about that.
I didn't think, when I was so kind as to take you out for
a bit of pleasure two or three nights, that it was going to
turn your head like this, and spoil the very qualities that
made me pity you. Look at this kitchen now! Look
at those dirty dishes! See the cat licking the roasting-
spit! See the yeast all working over the floor; and
the kettle not filled, although it's tea-time already!
Why, Cinderella, you're just as bad as your sisters, the
moment you get the chance. The only reason that you
have been patient, and industrous, and amiable so far, is
that you never have dreamed of anything beyond your

kitchen. The moment you are tempted to rebel, see how quickly you do it."

By this time, you may well believe, Cinderella was crying plentifully, and coming to her godmother, she fell upon her knees, kissed the old fairy's withered hand, and said :

"Pray forgive me, godmother. I see now how bad I have been; I never will do so any more; but please don't say that I shan't go to the prince's ball to-night."

"The prince's ball, indeed! Ha! ha! I guess so! Hum! Prince's fiddlestick's-end!" sniffed the fairy god-mother in high disdain. "If it was not for the ball, how sorry would you be for your naughtiness !"

"Oh, godmother, I don't know, because it *is* for the ball, and I can't forget it," sobbed Cinderella, who was, after all, a very truthful girl; but her godmother was not pacified even by this frankness, and pulling her hand away from Cinderella, began marching up and down the kitchen, muttering :

"Yes, yes, she needs a lesson—a pretty sharp one, too —or she will never do for the prince's wife. I'm not going to have her like the common run of queens, I can tell her. H'm, h'm—prince's ball—oh, yes, I dare say."

Toot! toot! Tra, la, la, tra, la, la! went a bugle in the court-yard, and the fairy godmother lifted her head sharply. "Go to the door, Cinderella!" said she.

Cinderella, wiping her red eyes upon her dirty apron,

did as she was bid, and in a few moments returned to the kitchen.

"Well, who was it?" demanded her godmother.

"A gentleman who asked to see the ladies: so I took him up to my sisters' drawing-room," replied Cinderella sadly.

"And why didn't you stay and see what he wanted of you?"

"He didn't want anything of me, godmother; he asked for the young ladies."

"Come, child, you are not entirely spoiled, and don't think yourself everybody quite yet," said the godmother, smiling grimly. "Come along with me to the drawing-room, and if those impertinent people in the corner wish to come too, they may."

"Oh ho, fairy godmother, you have found us out, have you?" laughed the Chimney-Elf. "Of course we're coming too, gossip: that's just what we're here for."

So the fairy godmother, leading Cinderella, and followed by Rhoda and the Chimney-Elf, went up into the grand drawing-room, where Finetta, the second sister, was already trying on the glass slipper, and doing her very best to squeeze her great toes into it, but without success. Suzette, the elder sister, sat on the sofa, looking very pale, and holding her foot in her hand. She had hurt it so dreadfully in her frantic efforts to get the slipper over her great heel that she could hardly keep from fainting.

"I am afraid the slipper is not intended for you Miss Finetta," said the gentleman courier, who stood watching the second sister's movements.

"There are no other young ladies in the house, I believe."

"Of course there are not," replied Finetta sharply, for she had been taken suddenly with cramps in the foot, and could not conceal her pain and mortification.

"My dears, you are growing old, and losing your memories," remarked the fairy godmother, coming forward. "Here is your younger sister, Cinderella, whom you have forgotten. Sit down and put on the slipper, child."

Cinderella, blushing and sparkling with delight, did as she was bid, put on the slipper, drew the mate to it from her pocket, and put that on too, and jumped up as easily as possible.

"Madam, the prince begs the honor of your hand in marriage, and prays you to accompany me at once to the palace," said the courier, going down upon his knees to kiss Cinderella's hand, and wishing that it had been a little cleaner. Before she could reply, the fairy godmother interrupted:

"Tell the prince that my goddaughter don't go running about the world looking for a husband. If he wants to marry her, he knows where to find her. You have your message, young man, and had better go

Cinderella, go down stairs and finish your work in the kitchen."

The courier looked extremely puzzled.

" Pardon me, madam," said he, bowing very low " But the prince said—"

" 'The prince said!' " retorted the fairy godmother. " What do you suppose I care what the prince said ? Go home, young man, and do your errand just as it was given you."

So the courier, looking very doubtful and awkward, was forced to go as he had come, and Cinderella very slowly and unwillingly put her glass slipper into her pocket, and went down to the kitchen again, followed by Suzette and Finetta, who were both sobbing out :

" Oh, 'Rella, don't you forget us when you are married to the prince, will you ? Let us come and help do the work, that's a dear ; and then we'll dress you all up in our best clothes, and you'll be ready for the prince whenever he comes. Oh, 'Rella, we always did love you dearly, and we ought to have been better sisters to you —we feel it now."

" There, stop that, and go to work, if you really mean what you say," interrupted the fairy godmother. " Suzette, go and draw water from the well, fill the teakettle and set it on; then bring coals from the cellar, make up the fire, and rake out the cinders. Finetta, get the tub and wash those dirty dishes; and Cinderella, sweep the kitchen, and put it in the nicest order directly."

The elder sisters, who never had done any hard or dirty work in their lives, were not at all pleased with these orders, but it would not do to disobey the fairy godmother; and above all things they wished to please Cinderella, who was about to become a princess. So they took off their lace undersleeves, pinned back their silken skirts, and went to work with the best grace they could. Cinderella meantime swept, and scrubbed, and set things in their places, so quickly and so well, that her godmother began to smile a little, and after about an hour said:

"There, child, run out into the wash-house and take a good bath, then come back to me to be dressed. The other girls can finish up the work."

Cinderella ran away, and returned after a while fresh, clean, and rosy, wrapped only in a great sheet. The fairy godmother waved her wand, and instantly she was dressed in the loveliest clothes imaginable, her hair beautifully arranged, and her feet covered by silk stockings with pink clocks, and the glass slippers.

"That'll do," said the fairy godmother, looking her all over. "The prince is just riding into the court yard."

CHAPTER XI.

THE CRUEL SPINDLE.

AS the fairy spoke, a great noise of trumpets, and horsemen, and running footmen announced the prince's arrival. The elder sisters, almost crying with vexation, washed and wiped their hands at the kitchen sink, and ran up stairs to change their dresses for the wedding.

The fairy, meantime having changed Cinderella's clothes into the most beautiful of bridal dresses, led her up to the great saloon, followed by Rhoda and the Chimney-Elf. Here, with one wave of her wand, she formed at the top of the room a lovely arch of evergreen, decorated with orange-flowers, white roses, lilies, and myrtle, with a carpet of white velvet underneath; and beneath this arch she placed Cinderella, who looked as lovely as the morning, but who dared not raise her eyes from the floor.

All this was but just arranged, when, with a great clatter of boot-heels and swords against the stone steps, the prince and his gentlemen mounted the staircase and entered the saloon. The fairy godmother went to meet them.

"Well, young man," said she to the prince, "so you want to marry Cinderella, do you? Now let me ask, why do you want to marry her?"

"Because she is the most charming young lady in the world," replied the prince, taking off his plumed hat and bowing, first to the fairy, and then to Cinderella.

"Stuff and nonsense," politely replied the fairy, taking snuff. "What do you know about her? What you marry her for is because she has the smallest foot in the kingdom, and wears glass slippers. Nice foundation glass slippers are for matrimonial happiness! I'm tired of the whole lot of you—good-by. Come along, Chimney-Elf."

And with two movements of her wand the fairy godmother turned the old claw-footed mahogany easy-chair beside her into a chariot drawn by a pair of griffins, pulled Rhoda and the Chimney-Elf into it, and flew out of the open window, just as the two sisters swept into the room dressed in their most gorgeous array.

8

"I haven't given her up, you understand," remarked the fairy godmother to Rhoda. "But young people do better to be left to themselves when they are first married. I shall look in upon them when the little prince comes, and if I am satisfied, I will do something handsome for him. I hope he won't vex me, though, as another god-child did—the Princess Dorma. Did you ever hear of her?"

"No, ma'am," replied Rhoda, holding tight to the side of the arm-chair, which jerked about very uncomfortably.

"I'll tell you all about it, then; for I am going there now, and it is always better to know something about people before you meet them, if it's only on which foot they have corns.

To begin with my dear Dorma's father: he was an old friend of mine; in fact, I was very fond of him, until he foolishly married the Fair One with the Golden Locks, vain, silly creature that she was; but I never could make him believe it. He would sit hour after hour twanging his stupid old guitar, singing love-songs to her, while she sat simpering and making eyes, and combing out her great yellow mane, to make it glitter in the sunshine, until that goose of a man didn't know whether he stood on his head or his heels. Well, I was vexed enough; but still I didn't give them up all at once, even after Dorma was born; but they forgot to ask me to the christening. I was a little hurt at that, I own, but all I did about it was to tell them to keep the child out of my turret of the palace; and another thing I told them was never to let her learn to spin, for as surely as she did she would come to grief."

" I should not think she would have cared much for that," remarked Rhoda.

" Bless you, child, did you ever go idle a whole day long? A woman who can't spin and is not allowed to do housework is like a three-legged kitten, or a lame-winged bird, or a candle without a blaze; she can't do what she was made to do."

" But I can't spin," persisted Rhoda.

" Pshaw, child! you can sew and knit, can't you! It's all the same thing, except that a hundred years ago, when all this happened, everybody spun more than they sewed or knit, and now they don't.

" Well, to make a long story short, I told them to keep Dorma out of my turret and away from a spinning-wheel: very well, they minded until the girl was about seventeen, when that stupid Fair One with the Golden Locks took it into her head to die. Dorma, being left to herself, and rather wretched at losing her mother, got in a way of wandering about the palace: at last, one unlucky day she found the key of my turret door, and let herself in. As ill-luck would have it, I was away, and had left my rock, and distaff, and spindle all in plain sight, with nobody to stop the little fool's meddling. So she seized upon the spindle the very first thing, and "'Oh!' she cried out 'what funny thing is this, and what is it good for, I wonder?'

"Now, my spindle, you must know, my dear, is an ill-tempered fairy, whom I keep shut up in that form, and compel her to spin yarns of various sorts for me, whenever the fancy takes me to call for one. This makes her cross, and finding herself rather rudely handled by poor little Dorma, she dug the end of the spindle into the child's hand, and hurt her so that she cried out dismally.

"I heard the cry, although I was some hundreds of miles away at the time, visiting my sister Pari-banou, so I flew to see what was the matter. A pretty sight met my eyes as I rushed in through the keyhole.

"There stood my poor little princess holding her bleeding hand tightly in the other, half crying, half frightened, and staring with all her eyes at Mistress Spindle, who was whirling around the room on her one foot, buzzing like an angry hornet, and making her flaxen hair fly out in a perfect cloud with the swiftness of her motion.

"I was so vexed that it made me unlady-like, and I am afraid I kicked the spindle into the corner of the room and called it names. Then I opened the door and whisked Dorma off to her own chamber, laid her upon the bed, and then, being determined to keep her quiet, if such a thing was possible, I just put her and the whole household, in fact everything in the palace,

fast asleep, and promised them a nap of a hundred years
at least. Then I flew off, and never have been near
them since. Now the hundred years are out; moreover,
I have undertaken to find a wife for Prince Charming,
a dear young friend of mine, and I think I shall bestow
Dorma upon him. A girl brought up as quietly as she
has been, cannot fail to make a good wife. Here we
are."

And the fairy godmother checked the griffins with a
motion of her hand, causing the arm-chair to remain
suspended above a thick and tangled wood, from the
midst of which rose the tall chimneys and turrets of a
castle.

Advancing toward this wood Rhoda perceived a
young man, brown, dusty, handsome, and eager, who
pressed forward toward the tangled forest so fast that
his retinue found it very hard to keep up with him. This
retinue, by the way, consisted of one man dressed in the
Highland costume, and holding a bagpipe under his arm,
upon which he played a single tune without ceasing.

> "'Over the hills and far away,
> Over the hills and far away!'
> And all the tune that he could play
> Was 'Over the hills and far away.'"

sang the fairy godmother, looking down and laughing.

"Well, my dear Charming, you will not complain,
when you see what I have brought you 'over the hills

and far away' to find. Hold tight, Rhoda! Hie away, griffins!"

And with a jerk, and a sweep, and a bounce, the arm-chair flew downward, and in at the open window of the fairy's own turret in the sleeping castle. Rhoda looked about her curiously, and soon discovered the disgraced spindle lying in the corner, where the fairy had kicked it a century before, a little dusty, to be sure, but otherwise quite ready to prick the fingers of any meddlesome girl who should disturb it.

"But those fingers won't be mine, you old thing," remarked she half aloud; and the fairy godmother, turning briskly round, exclaimed:

"I should hope not. A girl brought up as you have been, has the use of her hands better than a poor little princess, who never had the good luck of waiting upon herself. But come, let us get down and see Prince Charming wake Dorma. It ought to be a pretty sight."

So down the winding turret stairs, and through the long dim corridors, and the resounding halls, and the stately chambers, went the fairy godmother, with the Chimney-Elf flitting like a smoke-wreath beside her, Rhoda tripping after, wondering whether all this could indeed be real, or if she were asleep and dreaming.

Some of these corridors and halls were empty, save for the stately old furniture, and the tapestry swaying from the walls with such life-like motion, that Rhoda half thought the knights, and ladies, and horses, and hounds, and nymphs, and Cupids embroidered upon it were real people stepping down to greet her. But in other of these lonely and echoing passages they came upon the figures of courtiers, of servants, of gray-bearded councillors, or smiling ladies, each struck to sleep in the gesture of that moment when poor little forgotten Dorma wounded her hand with the forbidden spindle.

Once they passed through a hall filled with armed guards, two of whom stood with crossed halberds before the arched doorway of an inner room; but the fairy godmother, with a little derisive laugh, stooped beneath the halberds, and pushed open the guarded doors with the point of her wand.

"There's my old lover at the head of his table, my dear," said she to Rhoda. "A proper enough man, was he not?"

Rhoda timidly raised her eyes, and saw a splendidly appointed table, its dishes of gold, and silver, and crystal glittering in the sunlight that streamed through a great painted window at the end of the hall. Around this table sat several gentlemen, some of them old, and the rest in middle life. All were richly dressed, with faces wise and good, like those of men fit to be the councillors of a king. Each face wore a smile, subdued and respectful, but admiring; and were turned toward the head of the table, where in a golden chair sat the king, their master He was a man in the prime of life, with a stately form,

a proud dark face, and an air of royal grace. Leaning
back in his great chair, the fingers of one hand idly
tangled in his flowing beard, the other clasped around a
great golden goblet upon the table, he looked as if still
uttering the jest or story frozen upon his lips by the
fairy spell; and the smile in his dark eyes was the original copied so carefully by the eyes of every courtier
about the table.

"Those idiots have waited a long time for the point
of the king's story," remarked the fairy godmother,
casting a look of frowning contempt upon the scene;
then she added more softly:

"Oh, my king, I would have done better than this
for you, if you had not preferred the Fair One with the
Golden Locks to me, in the old days."

And so they passed through the banqueting room,
and the silent halls beyond, and up the great staircase
guarded by its enchanted sentries, and through more
halls and anterooms, until the fairy lifted a curtain of
soft blue silk, and passed with Rhoda and the elf into a
chamber more beautiful than anything they yet had seen.
It was better than beautiful, for it was filled with the

purity, and simplicity, and innocence that should make the chamber of a young girl different from any other. Upon an ivory bedstead in the centre of the room lay the princess, fast asleep, one hand beneath her cheek, the other closely folded like that of a little child in pain. The golden rippling hair, thrown back from the pure pale face, lay in great shining masses upon the blue silk counterpane; but the heavy eyelashes so closely folded over the great eyes were darker by many shades, as were the perfect brows above. About the little mouth, so curved and rosy, hung a tremulous pout, as if even in her long, long sleep, Dorma dreamed of the cruel spindle that had wounded her. Beneath the hem of her white and gold-embroidered robe peeped a little foot, its blue velvet shoe ornamented with the royal cipher in gold thread; while the open sleeve falling away from the wounded hand showed an arm of exquisite beauty circled by a bracelet of quaint device.

"Poor little lamb! your hand is quite well now; you had better guard your heart instead," murmured the fairy godmother, stooping over this lovely figure and smiling half kindly, half mournfully. Then rising, she drew Rhoda a little aside, saying quietly:

"Wait here, my dear. He never will look at us. Hark!"

Rhoda listened, and from the forest, whose tangled trees grew almost into the windows of the sleeping palace, she heard the shrill notes of the bagpiper still playing

"Over the hills and far away," but so faintly now, that it showed the piper to be well-nigh exhausted.

"He's had a long journey of it, poor fellow, but it's over now," said the fairy, nodding her head good-naturedly.

Rhoda, still listening, heard the hasty footsteps of the prince as he hurried through hall, and passage, and guard-room, up the great staircase and through the ante-room, until at last he paused before the silken curtain that shut in the chamber of the princess.

CHAPTER XII.

THE SLEEPING BEAUTY.

A MOMENT of silence followed, and then the prince with slow and trembling hands pulled aside the curtain, and peeped in. His eyes fell upon the sleeping figure of Dorma, and suddenly exclaiming, "It is the lady of my dreams!" he ran toward her, knelt beside the bed, and taking the little clenched hand in his, pulled it gently, as if to wake the sleeper; but still she slumbered on.

"Well, then!" exclaimed Prince Charming; and rising to his feet, he stooped, and pressed his lips upon the pale, beautiful cheek of the princess, while his own grew rosy red beneath its healthy brown.

"Oh!" murmured Princess Dorma; and then, for the first time in a hundred years, she unclosed her great blue eyes, and fixed them upon the dark ones of the prince.

"Sweetest!" said he, "I have wandered the whole world over to find you."

"And I have waited a hundred years for you to come, my prince," whispered Dorma, laying both her hands in his, and rising from her long, long nap.

But now began a bustle and confusion through the whole palace, as strange to listen to in that secluded place as the dead silence had been fearful. Doors slammed, the voices of page, and groom, and soldier mingled with the shrill tones of women and children, the neighing of horses and barking of dogs, in fact, every manner of sound to be expected in and about a great palace filled with attendants. Presently the curtains were drawn aside, and a starched, severe-looking lady, wearing a high cap of stiff muslin and a train four yards in length, appeared in the doorway. She was Madam Prunella Prisms, the princess' governess, and the horror of her life.

"His majesty, your royal highness' father, desires the pleasure—A-h-h-h! what do I see—a m-a-n!"

And Madam Prunella Prisms fainted dead away, and fell upon the floor, or rather upon her train, much to the injury of the stiff muslin cap, which got its crown most dreadfully mashed.

"Let us go to papa, then," said Dorma, laughing a

little at her governess' mishap. Then, hand in hand like
two loving children, they went, while down in the
court-yard the piper, now quite refreshed, struck shrilly
up his one tune of " Over the hills and far away."

" Yes, and she'll leave father, and home, and all, to
follow her prince 'over the hills and far away,' just
like the rest of them," grumbled the fairy godmother.
" Isn't it a blessing we fairies don't have children to
grow up and run away from us ? But come along,
Rhoda, and you too, Mr. Smoke-wreath ; I am going
now, and I will set you down wherever you like. Where
shall it be ? "

" If we might go with you, ma'am— " suggested
Rhoda, who had taken a great fancy to the fairy godmother.

" With me, child ? Well, I am going back to carry
this mischievous spindle as a wedding-present to Cinderella. She has got into trouble, and I must help her
out, by means of the spindle."

" How do you know she is in trouble ? " asked
Rhoda.

" How do I know ? Well, if I should tell you, you
would know as much as I do. But I will tell you something else much more amusing. After Cinderella was
married, she was so praised for her industry, and her
knowledge of useful arts, that she grew very proud, and
took to boasting that she could do this, and that, and the
other thing so much better and faster than any one else,

that finally no one believed her, and every one was laugh-ing at her. At last she declared before the whole court that she could spin the yarn and knit twelve pairs of stockings between sunset and sunrise, and have time for sleep besides. The queen, her mother-in-law, overheard this foolish boast, and wishing to mortify her, she took up the offer, and said:

" ' Come, then, my daughter, prove your words by doing what you say. Knit the stockings, and I will give you my set of diamonds in payment for them.'

" This was the time for Cinderella to confess her folly, and escape from the trap her mother-in-law had set for her ; but instead of that, the foolish girl persisted in her folly, and was marched away to a great store-room at the top of the palace, half filled with wool. A spinning-wheel was set before her, several sets of knitting-needles laid ready, and then the door was locked. The prince, her husband, was away from her at the time, or he never would have allowed this, of course. Poor Cin-derella, forlorn and frightened, sat down among the wool and began to cry. Suddenly, from the very middle of the pile, a little voice squeaked out :

" ' Don't cry, princess ; I'll spin and knit a dozen pairs of stockings for you before midnight, and you may lie down and go to sleep meantime.'

" ' Thank you very much ; but who are you, and where are you ?' asked Cinderella, looking all about her.

" ' Never mind that,' replied the voice. ' Go to sleep.'

" And to sleep she went sure enough, without more words. Early in the morning, the queen-mother, a little frightened at what she had done, came to let out her daughter-in-law, and found her still sleeping, but with the twelve pairs of stockings not only knitted, but beautifully washed, and pressed, and folded in order upon the table.

" ' Wonderful ! ' cried the queen, and the king, and the court ; and the whole nation cried ' Wonderful ' too, when they heard of it. At last came the prince, who, when he was told the story of his wife's industry, only laughed and shook his finger at her, and said :

" ' Oh, oh, you rogue ! I will never believe it until I see it. Knit a dozen pairs more to-night, and I will give you a dress of woven sunbeams.'

" ' Very well,' replied Cinderella, and, when night came, shut herself up in the store-room, and called upon her little friend among the wool to help her. But he sulkily answered that he could not work without wages, and that he had not yet been paid for his first dozen pairs of stockings.

" ' Well, what shall I pay you ? ' asked Cinderella, wondering if she must give up the queen's diamonds as soon as she got them.

" ' What shall you give me ? ' repeated the voice. ' Oh, not very much. You shall give me—well, your first child when it is a month old. If you will agree to that,

I will promise to knit all the stockings you ask for between this day and that.'

"Well, my dear, Cinderella consented—very wrong of course; but still she did it, and the stockings were knitted, and a great number of dozens more, of various twines, until one pleasant day the princess became the mother of a fine boy. The whole country was filled with rejoicing; every one was happy but the mother, poor Cinderella, who began too late to think of her bargain with the stocking-knitter. When the month came round, she shut herself and the baby up in her own chamber, and held him tight in her arms, determined to fight for him to the last. All at once she heard the squeaky little voice saying:

"'Well, princess, I have come for the baby. You may carry him into the spinning-chamber, and lay him down on the heap of wool out of which I have spun you so many stockings, then leave the room and lock the door.'

"But Cinderella cried, and begged, and argued, and promised all sorts of things, and went on at such a rate that finally the voice replied peevishly:

"'Oh, well, do stop this fuss, and I'll tell you what I will do. One month from this hour, you shall tell me my name, and promise never to ask me to knit for you any more, or you shall give me the baby, and yourself into the bargain. I could make you into a Spinning-jenny, I think.'

"So Cinderella promised as usual—it is so easy for some people to make promises—and the danger was over for that time. But now the month has come round again, and at this very moment poor Cinderella is sitting in her own room with the little prince in her arms, crying her heart out: just now she was calling for me to help her; did not you hear her?"

"No, ma'am," replied Rhoda, staring about her at the clouds and mountain-tops among which the arm-chair was now floating.

"Well, I did," said the fairy dryly. Shaking her whip over the griffins' ears, she made them step out at such a rate that in another moment they reached and alighted upon the roof of a great palace. The window of a turret stood open, and the fairy godmother stepped into it without the ceremony of knocking. Rhoda and the Chimney-Elf followed. Just inside, the fairy stopped, and taking a box hollowed from a single diamond out of her pocket, she opened it and threw a little of the greenish dust it contained into Rhoda's face, saying at the same time:

"There, child, you are invisible now; this is fern-seed dust, and as good as the Mantle of Darkness, besides being more portable. Now you can go about anywhere and no one will see you, though you see them. Smoke-wreath and I can make ourselves invisible without it, merely by wishing."

"But I can see you, ma'am," said Rhoda, "and I can see Smoke-wreath too."

9

"Of course you can," the fairy replied, "because we don't wish you not to see us. But we must not lose time talking here. So now come along."

So the fairy led, and Rhoda followed through corridors, and down stairs, and through chamber after chamber, until they reached a locked door, which, however, opened at a touch of the fairy's wand, and admitted them to a splendid room, even more splendid than that of the Princess Dorma. In the middle of the room sat Cinderella upon a throne-chair of blue velvet, with a great gold crown suspended over it, and a golden footstool in front of it. In her arms she held a lovely baby and both she and the child were dressed in the richest lace, and embroidery, and purple, and fine linen; but, in spite of all these pleasant things about her, Cinderella was crying bitterly; and the little child looking up at her with great frightened eyes, had put up his little lips as if about to cry also.

"Well, my dear, how do you find yourself to-day?" asked the fairy godmother, quietly taking a seat and making herself visible to Cinderella, who started and cried out:

"Oh, how you frightened me, and how glad I am to see you, godmother! I am so unhappy!"

"Dear me, you're always unhappy, it seems to me. What's the matter now?"

But at this simple question Cinderella began to blush, and hang her head, and stammer all sorts of

nonsense; for how could she tell her godmother of the
foolish and boastful lies that had first led her into
trouble, and how could she answer without telling of
them? So she blundered along as people do who are
afraid to speak the truth, until the fairy stopped her
with a contemptuous wave of the hand:

"There, there, that will do, princess. I know all
about it better than you do; only I wanted to see
whether you had the courage to tell me the true story.
It seems you have not, so you had better hold your
tongue."

Cinderella hung her head and was silent; but the
great tears rolled down her cheeks and fell upon the
baby's face, so that his poor little lips began to tremble
more than ever. The fairy stood looking at the two for
several minutes very severely, but at last her face soft-
ened, and she said, not unkindly:

"Well, you goose, are you going to let Rumplestilt-
kins have the baby?"

"Rumple—oh, godmother, is that his name?" cried
Cinderella, jumping off the throne and rushing up to
the fairy, who took a pinch of rose-pollen snuff, and dryly
inquired:

"Is what whose name?"

"Why, the knitting man—the horrid wretch who
wants the baby. I have to tell him his name to-day, or
he will take us both away. Oh, godmother—oh, I don't
want to be made into a Spinning-jenny."

"Don't you? Well, then, his name is Rumplestilt-kins, and you can tell him I said so, if you like. So that's all settled, and now good-by."

"Oh, stop a minute, please, dear godmother. There's one thing more," exclaimed Cinderella, turning very red again. "The king wants me to knit some more stockings for nim, to give as a present to the Khan of Grand Tartary, who has sent a special ambassador to ask if I would oblige him so much. And I promised Rumple-stiltkins that I never would ask him to do any more, and—and—I can't knit at all."

"Then, why, pray, did you ever say that you could?" asked the fairy, severely. "You deserve to suffer for your wicked folly, and I am glad you do; and although I am going to help you out of this scrape, I will never do so again unless you amend, so far at least as to tell the truth. Take this spindle, put it in the wool-chamber, and say to it:

> ' Spindle straight, and spindle true,
> Here's some work for you to do;
> Turn and twist the magic thread
> Until the task shall all be sped.'

Then come out and leave it as many hours as you wish pairs of stockings, and when you go back they will be ready. But, remember whenever you touch it, that I have given it orders to wound your hands as often as you have told wrong stories since you last handled it, and I assure you it will obey me sharply enough.

There, that will do—I am not very fond of kissing.
Good-by, and mind that you tell your husband all about
this before you sleep to-night. He will give you a
sound scolding, and it will be good for you."

So saying, the fairy godmother became invisible, and
glided out of the room, followed by Rhoda and the
Chimney-Elf, neither of whom had Cinderella been able
to perceive at all.

RUMPLESTILTKINS.

CHAPTER XIII.

SIR LANCELOT DU LAC.

"AND now, my dear, we must part company," remarked the fairy godmother as she checked the griffins in the midst of a thick forest. "Cinderella will do very well after she has received two or three sharp hints from her friend the spindle; and poor little Dorma and her prince will be as happy as two geese in a goose-pond, for a while at least. I must go now and attend to some other friends of mine; so good-by, and good luck to you, child; and if you would like the box of fern-seed, here it is." 134

"But, ma'am!" began Rhoda, and then stopped, finding herself alone, with only the little diamond box at her feet to prove that the fairy had ever been with her.

"Isn't she queer, Chimney-Elf!" cried Rhoda, staring about her. No one replied, and Rhoda stared still harder. Could it be that the Chimney-Elf had deserted her? She called his name loudly and repeatedly, but only the wind sighing through the pine-trees and the crows flying far over her head replied. The moody little elf had grown jealous of Rhoda's interest in the fairy and her friends, and had either taken himself off, or rendered himself invisible, and refused to reply to her entreaties.

"Oh, dear, dear, what shall I do now?" exclaimed the poor child, sinking down upon the root of a great tree, and looking despairingly about her. As she did so, the tramp of a horse's feet became audible in the distance, and in another moment Rhoda perceived the glittering figure of a knight in full armor, mounted upon a large black war-horse, slowly riding up the avenue of arching trees, beneath which the fairy had dropped her. He did not at first perceive her, and Rhoda examined both knight and war-horse with a sort of frightened curiosity, for although she had read of such beings in her story-books, she had never seen anything of the sort. The knight had taken his helmet off and hung it at his saddle-bow, so that Rhoda perceived him to be both handsome and young, with a dark complexion, bold black eyes, and curling black hair falling to his shoulders. His armor was of polished steel curiously inlaid with blue enamel; the waving plume upon his helmet was also blue; and whenever throughout his dress or equipments any color was allowed to appear, that color was sure to be blue. The only exception to this rule was a scarlet sleeve embroidered with pearls, which was bound upon the front of his helmet, contrasting richly with the azure plume. The horse was also in armor, but he paced along beneath his caparisons of blue and steel with an ease that showed both strength and training. As the knight rode he sang in a clear deep voice, " Tirra lirra, lirra, lirra," and hummed the song of which this was the refrain, between his closed lips. As the black horse came opposite the place where Rhoda was sitting, he swerved suddenly aside, so that the knight swayed in his saddle, and catching at the loose rein, cried angrily :

" Hold there, Tonnerre! what is it now?" Glancing around as he spoke, he caught sight of the child, and checking Tonnerre altogether, he sat looking at her in astonishment for a moment; then leaping from the horse, he approached, saying in his strong deep voice :

" How now, my little maid? Art in the forest here alone?"

Rhoda, thus addressed, rose to her feet, and blushing brightly, replied:

"Yes, sir; the fairy godmother left me here, and then the Chimney-Elf ran away."

"So you are a child of the fairies! I too have a fairy godmother. Morgana, the Lady of the Lake, will welcome you. But who is the Chimney-Elf, and how came he and thy godmother to desert thee so cruelly!"

"Oh, she is not my godmother, but Cinderella's," replied Rhoda simply.

"Cinderella's!" repeated the knight in a puzzled voice. "Well, well, I do not understand thy prattle; but I know those who will be right glad to talk with thee. Come, let me put thee upon Tonnerre's neck, and take thy way with me; for certes I will not leave thee alone in the wood, nor can I tarry longer here. Come, little one."

As he spoke, he drew off his steel gauntlet, and offered his right hand to Rhoda, who laid her own in it without hesitation, and suffered herself to be led to the side of the great black war-horse, and lightly sprang up to a seat in front of the saddle, without a thought of fear or resistance. The knight mounted behind her, and holding her firmly with one arm, he gathered up the reins and spoke to Tonnerre, who pranced a little under the double load, but presently fell into a gentle amble, and passing on through sun and shade, carried his riders far along the forest road that led to Camelot.

"And now, little maid, tell me thy name!" asked the knight presently; and Rhoda, obeying him, added in a hesitating voice, "I should like to know your name too, if you please, sir."

"Men call me Lancelot du Lac. Didst ever hear the name?" replied the knight, smiling pleasantly.

"No, sir—yes—I read about him once in a book, and King Arthur, and the Round Table; but that was not a true story, I think, though it was as true as Cinderella, and The Sleeping Beauty, and Red Riding-Hood—"

"I know nothing of all these," replied the knight, smiling still. "But I know for a truth that I am Lancelot du Lac, and that my lord King Arthur is real, and that the Round Table is the centre of the fairest gathering of knights that ever came together. You shall see it at Camelot, whither we are going."

"Are we going to Camelot, now?" asked Rhoda.

"Yes, pretty one, as fast as Tonnerre will carry us. The king and queen and all the court are there, and there will be feasts, and jousting, and music, and dancing, and all kinds of merry-making. That will please thee, will it not?"

"I suppose so, sir; but are there any other little girls at Camelot?"

Lancelot smiled; but before he could reply the conversation was interrupted by a piercing shriek in a woman's voice, followed by the sound of crashing branches and hasty footsteps.

"Soho! what is this?" exclaimed Sir Lancelot, checking Tonnerre, and hastily replacing his helmet upon his head. He had hardly done so when out from a narrow side-path rushed a lady, her clothes torn and soiled, her hair streaming, and her face pale and blood-streaked. Seeing Lancelot, she uttered a sobbing cry of delight and sprang toward him.

"Sir Lancelot du Lac! oh, save me, noble knight, save me from the wretch who has just murdered my husband, and would now murder me, who never did him harm, or wished him ill!"

"Rest you easy, lady—stand there behind me, and guard this child—I will do the rest!" hastily replied the knight, placing Rhoda upon the ground, laying his lance in rest, and wheeling Tonnerre's head toward the opening in the trees, through which now rushed a man with drawn sword in hand, and blood upon his rusty armor. His helmet was upon his head, and the lowered visor hid his face; but by the bearings upon the little shield he carried on his left arm, Sir Lancelot recognized and addressed him:

"What, Guy du Fontaine, it is thou! and at thine old work! What knight but thou would pursue a lady with a naked sword in his hand, and her lord's blood upon his armor? Stand and answer to me."

"And thou in saddle and with lance in rest, and I on foot with only sword and shield! Such is the bravery of the Round Table!" exclaimed the stranger knight in a harsh, forbidding voice, and with a scornful laugh. Sir Lancelot replied by leaping to the ground and placing

Tonnerre's rein in the hand of the lady who stood trembling beside him.

"If you see me coming by the worst, fair lady, mount my steed and save thyself. He will take thee to Camelot before sunset, and there shalt thou find protection for thyself and an avenger for me. Stay; I will place thee in the saddle with the child in front of thee, lest you might be unable to mount alone. Put thy foot in my hand, and—so! Now, little maid, it is thy turn; and lady, if once you see me down, ride away, and leave me to my fate. Heaven keep thee."

"And Heaven keep thee, gentle knight, and send thee victory—"

"And am I to stand waiting until thou makest thy last will, and sayest good-by to all thy lady-loves, thou squire of dames?" demanded Sir Guy impatiently.

"Guard thyself, false knight, and God defend the right!" exclaimed Sir Lancelot, whirling his sword above his head, and springing lightly forward. The other threw himself into position to receive the attack, the two swords clashed together, and the fight began. Never a knight of Arthur's court could call himself the superior of Sir Lancelot at any knightly exercise, and but few had ever gained advantage of him; but this Sir Guy du Fontaine was one of the most accomplished swordsmen of France, and to-day he fought with fierce determination for the victory: while Sir Lancelot's mind was disturbed by the feeling that the lady and Rhoda were exposed to danger should he fall, and also by his efforts to keep between them and their enemy, lest the latter should suddenly rush upon and attack them. The consequence of this divided attention was that a huge downward blow from Sir Guy's heavy Milan blade cut through the armor protecting Sir Lancelot's left arm, and inflicted a sharp if not dangerous wound.

"Ha, boaster! yield thee—thy blood flows fast!" exclaimed Du Fontaine; but Lancelot replied:

"Wait until we see thy blood also, before we speak of yielding. On guard!"

And again the bright swords clashed, and the knights rushed upon each other, while the sunbeams through the branches fell upon the polished armor of the one, and the dark figure of the other, upon the great black war-horse, and the frightened lady, and Rhoda with her wondering eyes and pale cheeks. And now Sir Lancelot, giving his whole attention to the conflict, pressed his opponent with such vigorous and well-directed blows, that the movements of the latter became hurried and unsteady, then faltering and aimless, until finally, with one great stroke, Sir Lancelot beat him to his knee. Standing over him, he drew the short dagger called "Misericordia," used by knights to finish combats begun with the sword. Holding this to his throat and preventing him from rising, Sir Lancelot exclaimed:

"Now yield thee, Guy du Fontaine, rescue or no rescue, passing me thy knightly word, that neither now

nor at any other time, shall this lady come to harm
through thee. Whatever cause of offence her lord may

have given thee has been avenged, and no knight wars
upon women. Speak, then!"

And by way of pointing his demand, Sir Lancelot
clicked the point of his dagger against the edge of the
other's cuirass, between which and the gorget the fatal
wound of the Misericordia was given.

"Enough! Thou hast me at advantage, and I yield,"
muttered Sir Guy sullenly, accepting the hint.

"And your pledge to respect the lady now and forever."

"Well—yes—I pass my word for her safety."

"It is enough; rise and go thy way, remembering,
that shouldst thou forget that pledge at any time, one
stands ready to recall it to thy mind."

Without reply the conquered knight slowly regained
his feet, picked up the sword that had flown far out of
his hand, and turning his back, made off without a word.
Sir Lancelot watched him out of sight, then slowly

crossed the little glade toward Tonnerre, who with his double burden stood awaiting him; but just before he reached the spot, a crashing among the undergrowth startled the spirited horse, who sprang forward and galloped down the path, while a furious wild boar rushed out from the thicket and made for Sir Lancelot.

The knight gave one hasty glance in the direction of Tonnerre's headlong flight; but seeing the impossibility of overtaking him upon foot, he turned his attention to the boar, whose movements 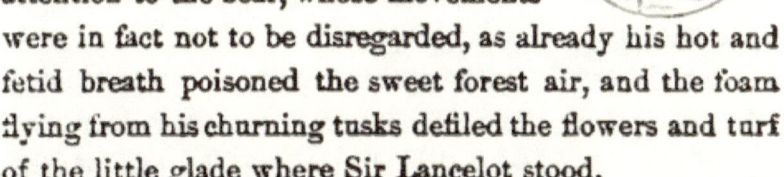 were in fact not to be disregarded, as already his hot and fetid breath poisoned the sweet forest air, and the foam flying from his churning tusks defiled the flowers and turf of the little glade where Sir Lancelot stood.

"Vile brute! Must I then stain my noble blade with thy life!" muttered the knight, drawing his sword and springing back a step, for already the powerful beast had aimed a blow of his tusks at the advanced foot of the knight, and as he sprang aside dashed headlong past, with such fury as to roll upon the ground in missing the expected resistance. Before he could recover, Sir Lancelot had sprung to his side, and dealt him a downright blow that should have slain any creature less fully protected than the boar; but from his armor-like hide the good sword slipped harmless. In the same instant the boar was upon his feet again, and, rushing upon the knight, avoided the point of the sword, so held that it would have entered his open mouth, swerved suddenly aside, and not heeding the edge of the blade, which slid harmlessly along his cheek, he aimed a blow with his tusks at the knight's right leg, which only the armor covering it prevented from taking full effect. As it was, Sir Lancelot staggered several paces, and had not recovered himself when the boar, turning short in his tracks, rushed upon him from behind, aiming to over-throw him and so be able to reach a more vulnerable point. The movement was so sudden and so unex-pected as almost to succeed, and Sir Lancelot, dropping upon one knee, let fall his sword, and seizing the dagger in his right hand, received the boar upon his wounded left arm, and at the same moment struck a deep and downright blow into the gleaming right eye of the creature, who, uttering a savage cry of rage and pain, threw himself forward, tearing and grinding with his tusks, which slid along the arm as far as the elbow, and there penetrating the point of the brassarde or armor of the arm, tore off the plate and inflicted a slight wound upon the flesh beneath. The next instant the boar rolled over in his death-agony, and Sir Lancelot, shaking himself free from the huge carcass, rose to his feet and looked about him.

The sun was near its setting, and its last rays struck through and through the treetops, casting a green and golden light into the depths of the forest, lighting them like noonday. All the birds had come home to their nests, and their evening songs filled the whole air; but except sights and sounds like these, Sir Lancelot saw and heard nothing. Tonnerre with his double burden was already far away, and Sir Guy du Fontaine had mounted his own horse and ridden as fast as he could from the scene of his defeat, so that the Knight of the Lake found himself as much alone in the wood as if he had been a hermit.

"I e'en must walk if I would go at all then," said he, smiling grimly, as he gathered up sword and dagger and replaced them in their sheaths. "Lucky it is that Master Boar has left me mine own legs, since Tonnerre no longer lends me his."

With these words, Sir Lancelot set forward at a good pace, and was soon lost in the depths of the forest. But rapidly though he might walk, how could a man hope to overtake a horse, especially Tonnerre, who, rejoicing in his unusual freedom, made the most of it by trotting, galloping, pacing, or walking at his own pleasure. His poor frightened riders made no attempt to control him, contenting themselves with clinging tight to the saddle and to each other, screaming for help at intervals. Rhoda was the first to recover from her terror and look about her. She found that the road along which they travelled was no longer a mere wood-path, that the forest was changing to scattered trees, between which she caught glimpses of a river running through green meadows and fields yellow with grain, and beside villages

10

whose white houses gleamed brightly in the rays of the setting sun.

"Oh, see, we are coming to a town, and there we shall find some one to help us," said she to her companion, who, clinging still closer to the horse's mane, sobbed out:

"We shall never come so far alive—we shall be dashed to pieces long before."

"I don't believe it," replied Rhoda stoutly. "The horse goes a little slower already, and we can stay on as well as we have done, I'm sure. Don't feel so scared, ma'am."

"You do not know of what you are talking, child," returned the lady impatiently. "But look, what comes down the hill yonder?"

She pointed as she spoke toward a turn of the road almost hidden by trees, among whose leaves could be seen the flashing of armor, the waving of pennons, and the forms of mounted men.

"I think they are more gentlemen like the one we left in the wood," said Rhoda timidly.

"Like Sir Lancelot du Lac!" exclaimed the lady, scornfully. "Let me tell you, girl, there are no more men like him, gentle or simple. But these may be his comrades, King Arthur's knights—yes, see, there is the standard of the dragon displayed as they come out into the sunshine. The king himself is with them, and we are safe!"

But at this moment Tonnerre perceived his com
rades in the distance, and throwing up his head with a
movement that almost unseated his riders, he uttered a
shrill neigh, and galloped forward to meet them. Seeing him coming, the party of knights halted, and sat
looking at the strange spectacle presented by the flying
steed and clinging riders.

"By my faith," exclaimed
Sir Percivale, who rode on
the king's right hand, "that
looks like Tonnerre, our
brother Lancelot's charger!"

"And so it does," added
Sir Gawain, the king's cousin.
"But what riders does he
bear? I know that Sir Lancelot du Lac is ever the
knight of dames, but—"

"Spare your wonder, messieurs," interposed the
king; "for another moment will show the truth. Ride
forward, Sir Galahad and Sir Percivale, and meet these
ladies."

The two knights, whom all men at Arthur's court
knew for the best and purest of those who sat at the
Round Table, rode forward at once, the silver armor of
Sir Galahad glittering in the last red light of day, and
the fair face of Sir Percivale smiling and gay. A few
moments brought the two parties together, and Tonnerre, touching his nose to that of Sir Galahad's white

charger, whinnied a joyous greeting and stopped short, while the knight, leaping to the ground, exclaimed:

"The Lady Isolde, and without her brave lord, Sir Ralph of Escourt! What chance is this, fair lady?"

"Sir Galahad, right glad am I to see you, and you too, fair Sir Percivale, for full well do I know that with you I am safe, and that the noble lord of whom you speak shall not die unavenged, for you were his friends."

The tears she could not restrain choked her voice, and covering her face with her hands she sobbed piteously. Sir Galahad and Sir Percivale sadly bowed their heads, and Sir Percivale softly said:

"And is it so, lady? Is our dear friend and brother-in-arms Sir Ralph gone from among us? But comfort you, dear lady, for well do I know that he died bravely and in the path of honor, as a good knight should, and to what other end do any of us look?"

"And trust us, fair Isolde, if he hath been foully dealt with, he shall not die unavenged," added Sir Galahad. "Who was his enemy?"

"Sir Guy du Fontaine. They quarrelled about a page who ran away from Sir Guy's cruel usage, and took refuge with us. Sir Ralph sheltered him, and refused to give him up at Sir Guy's command; so Sir Guy laid in wait for us, as we rode toward Camelot, and he slew my dear lord: if it had not been for good Sir Lancelot, he had slain me also!"

" And where is Sir Lancelot now, and who is this little maid, and how came you by Tonnerre ? " asked Sir Galahad, unable longer to restrain the questions he had been longing to ask. But before the lady could reply, Sir Percivale spoke:

" Here comes our lord the king: had not the Lady Isolde better tell her story to him rather than to us ? "

" To him and to you together; for though the king is chief of his knights, Sir Galahad and Sir Percivale are chief among knights," said the lady, bowing courteously.

And now King Arthur himself rode up, and Rhoda, looking at him with great wondering eyes, beheld a tall and stately man, dressed in armor richly inlaid with gold, with a crown wrought around his helmet, and wearing for crest the dragon of his father Uther, surnamed Pendragon. At his side glittered the jeweled hilt of the sword Excalibur, given him by the mysterious Lady of the Lake, the foster-mother of Sir Lancelot; upon one side of the blade was engraven in the oldest of old languages the command, " Take me ! " and upon the other appeared in the language of whoever looked at it, the words, " Cast me away ! " Not even Merlin, the wise man of Arthur's court, could explain the meaning of these contradictory phrases, but all agreed in saying that Excalibur was gifted with magic power, and that it was by its aid that Arthur had so easily proved victor in every battle where he had personally fought.

But after the first glance, Rhoda looked neither at the golden armor, nor the dragon crest, nor Excalibur, but fixed her eyes upon the face of the king, which seemed to her more beautiful than the face of man, with its bright blue eyes, and golden hair and beard, and the look of strength, and nobleness, and goodness which beamed from every line. As he approached, the knights drew back a little, and the Lady Isolde would have dismounted to offer her homage, but the king prevented her. He spoke a few courteous words of welcome in a voice so full of majesty and sweetness, not without a touch of sadness, that all little Rhoda's heart went out to him, and she would have given much to kiss his hand as did the Lady Isolde, who insisted upon thus rendering her homage.

Then the king asked the meaning of the lady's strange plight, and she told her story, and how all that she knew of Rhoda was the finding her with Sir Lancelot in the wood; but the king, looking kindly at the child, said:

"Do not fear, my little maid, but that your friend Sir Lancelot will find you out right soon; meantime you shall with this lady be the guest of my wife, Dame Guinevere, who waits for us at Camelot. Sir Percivale, shall the demoiselle ride with you? And Lady Isolde, can you content yourself upon Tonnerre for another mile or so?"

And as neither knight nor lady objected to these arrangements, the change was made, and the troop rode gayly on to Camelot.

CHAPTER XIV.

CAMELOT.

BENEATH the clear light of a full moon, King
Arthur and his knights, with the lady and the
child in their midst, rode into the beautiful old town
of Camelot. They clattered through the narrow streets,
where the stone fronts of the houses, leaning toward
each other, were so carved with dragons, and griffins,
and curious monsters, mingled with cherubs, and saints,
and strange dim devices, that it seemed as if the very
walls were alive and moving. From the balconied windows looked ladies and children, and the streets were
full of knights and men-at-arms; the most of them

dressed in silk, or cloth, or leather, having laid aside
their heavy armor to enjoy the cool of the evening.
Ever as the troop rode on the cry arose, "Here comes
the king, our noble and beloved king! God bless King
Arthur, and the Knights of the Round Table!"

And the king, turning his face this way and that,
smiled back a greeting like that of a father to his children. Rhoda, watching him, wished that she too might
call him king, and live forever in his sight.

So through the town the troop passed on until they
reached a hill, in the midst of which Merlin had built a
palace for the king, so wonderful and so magnificent
that all the people from far and near crowded to look at
it and take pride in it. In the centre was a hall lighted
by twelve great windows, each one painted with the
story of one of the twelve great battles fought and won
by Arthur in combat with the heathen who filled the
land when he became king, and whom he subdued and
banished. Besides these twelve windows was another
at the east, pictured with the story of the finding of
Excalibur; and another opposite it at the west, where
was shown that last great battle upon the sea-shore,
where Arthur met his rebellious knights headed by his
kinsman Modred, and where the strength and flower of
the Round Table fell by each other's hand.

In this battle it was that the king received the
grievous hurt of which some men say he died; but
others know that a great boat was waiting for him upon

the shore, wherein were the three queens who were his friends and sisters; and that he, with them, sailed away and away to the Island of Avilion, which lies within the splendors of the moon.

Under the sculptured gateway and through the great court rode the knights and ladies. They dismounted at the wide open doors of the palace, beside which stood armed warders, their weapons lowered respectfully in presence of the king. Sir Percivale lifted Rhoda from his horse, and taking her by the hand, led her forward into the hall, saying pleasantly:

"Come then, little one, thou shalt be my fair lady for this day, and evening, if thou wilt, for there is to be a feast, and after that music and dancing. Every knight is mated with a lady who is to be his chief companion and charge throughout the whole. Wilt thou honor me so far?"

"Thank you, sir," replied Rhoda timidly; "if the king is willing, I shall be very happy to sit with you."

"Well said, my little maid. The king first always; though much I marvel that thou so soon hast learned our ways. And what may I call thee?"

"Rhoda, if you please, sir."

"Rhoda? That means a rose, and thou shalt bestow upon me a rose from out this vase, and I, wearing it, shall show to all men that I and none other am thy chosen knight."

"Very well, sir; if you like, I will give you a rose, though it is not mine to give; and I don't know whether the king would like to have me take flowers out of his vases," replied Rhoda so gravely that Sir Percivale laughed aloud. Leading her close to one of the great dragon vases that stood all around the hall, he said:

" Fear nothing, most obedient of subjects. The king permits more than such a theft as this, to a lady."

So encouraged, Rhoda pulled a beautiful half-blown rose from the vase, and shyly gave it to Sir Percivale, who took it with a low bow, saying:

" When I have left thee with our lady the queen, I shall go to my own lodgings and change this heavy armor for a silken doublet, and upon the breast of it I shall clasp thy token, as thou wilt see."

At this moment a page dressed in the queen's livery approached, and bowing reverently to Sir Percivale, said :

"I am sent by my lord the king to lead this lady to the queen's apartments, whither he has already gone with the Lady Isolde of Escourt."

" That is well; and I will conduct thee as far as the door, my little Rhoda, before I go to mine own apartment," said Sir Percivale, offering his hand, in which Rhoda placed her own. So conducted, and led by the page, she passed on through the hall, and up a wide, richly carved staircase to a sumptuous chamber, where upon a chair of state sat Queen Guinevere, the loveliest woman of her time. Her bower-maidens were standing at her back, and Lady Isolde seated upon a low stool near at hand, while the king, leaning upon his sheathed sword, stood talking gayly with them both.

As Rhoda entered the door and paused, uncertain what to do next, the king came forward, and taking her by the hand, led her to the queen, saying:

"Here, dame, is our Lancelot's little friend. Be good to her for his sake, and her own, and mine."

"For all sakes she is welcome," replied the queen graciously, extending her hand to Rhoda, who placed her own in it, as in the act of shaking hands, then withdrew it; the queen looked surprised, the Lady Isolde smiled scornfully, and the king said:

"Dost not thou care to kiss the queen's hand when it is given thee, little one?"

"Oh!—I didn't know she wanted me to," replied Rhoda, blushing scarlet, and trying to regain the hand she had dropped; but the queen, withholding it, coldly said:

"You are excused, demoiselle. No doubt you come from some heathen land where such observances are unknown. And so, Isolde, thou didst leave Sir Lancelot fighting with a wild boar?"

The lady replied, and neither took further notice of Rhoda until the king said:

"Dame Guinevere, wilt not thou give orders to one of these thy maidens, to see what our little guest may need in the way of rest, refreshment, or garments? She will sit at the feast with us to-night, I trust."

"If she likes, most certainly, my lord," replied the queen, beckoning to one of the bower-maidens. "You heard the king's orders, Alicia; see that they are obeyed."

"Yes, your majesty," replied the girl, signing to Rhoda to follow her; but again the king interfered:

"And we shall see thee in the hall to-night, fair lady?"

"Yes, sir: the gentleman you call Sir Percivale asked me to sit beside him at the table, and he—" began Rhoda and stopped confused, for the two ladies were staring at her with such strange looks that she feared to have said something wrong.

"Sir Percivale chose thee for his lady at the feast and in the dance, child!" exclaimed the queen at last.

"Yes, ma'am; and he is going to wear a rose as a sign that it is so, because my name is Rhoda, and he says that means a rose," said the child, trembling at her own daring.

"I had intended to give Sir Percivale to Ygonde the Fair, and Sir Galahad to thee, Isolde," exclaimed the queen pettishly. "He might at least have asked thy pleasure, my lord, even though mine was of no account."

"Nay then, dame, I think he hath chosen well enow," replied the king smiling. "Thou wilt not marry thy favorite Ygonde with my Sir Percivale just yet; and our little guest, Rhoda, since that is her name, will have for this evening at least a knight of whom no one can speak an evil word."

So saying, he made a gesture of dismissal. Rhoda followed her guide to a chamber, where with fresh water, ivory combs, and a silken mantle which Alicia insisted upon throwing over her shoulders, she made so great an improvement in her appearance, that when shortly after she was conducted to the withdrawing room where the knights waited for their ladies, Sir Percivale, in offering her his hand, and pointing to the rose in his doublet, said :

" Is the flower named from thee, or art thou named from the flower, fairest rose of roses ? "

"Oh, if you please, don't talk that way to me, Sir Percivale," exclaimed Rhoda in real distress. " I am only a little girl, and never saw any gentleman like you in the world—that is, in the world I used to live in ; but here everything is different, and I don't quite know— "

" Did you come from that strange dim world that they tell us we all used to live in ? Sometimes I remember like a dream that I was not always here," said Sir Percivale thoughtfully. " But after all, this is the real life, and that was only a vision ; so let it pass, dear little Rhoda, and we will take our places at the table. It is fairly laid, is it not ? "

As he spoke he led Rhoda forward into the hall, which was now brilliantly lighted by great wax candles set in golden candlesticks shaped like trees, all down the long tables which stretched across the lower end of the hall, and which were now covered with the preparations for a feast of the grandest description. At the upper end of each table stood a peacock, roasted, and then re-dressed in his own feathers and head, so that he looked as if alive.

Below were kids, little pigs, and lambs, all whole, and so arranged as to look as much like life as possible. Besides these were dishes of such dainties as stewed snails, mullets stewed in red wine carrying smaller fishes in their mouths, deer's brains, and various other prepara-rations not now found or heard of at any table.

The only vegetables presented were boiled greens in two or three varieties, and wild cresses and salads; with them were cakes of fine wheaten bread called manchets, and only used in Arthur's time by the richest people, the poorer classes eating coarse black bread filled with the husks of the grain and nearly as hard as a stone.

At intervals along the board stood gigantic pies or pastries twelve or fourteen inches high, ornamented all over with flowers, fruits, or animals made of pastry, and filled with varieties of birds, with hares, pork, or venison. Fruit from the royal gardens and sweet cakes stood ready for the dessert, and great flagons of wine and beer were flanked by tankards of Mead and Metheglin, intended for the weaker heads of the ladies.

These tables thus loaded filled the lower half of the hall; in the upper half, raised by a step and called the dais, stood the famous Round Table, made by Merlin or by the spirits whom he knew how to compel to obey him. Around the edge of this table were carved the stories of the great combats fought by Arthur and his knights against both men and beasts, while the top was beautifully inlaid with various colored woods arranged in designs not to be understood save by those to whom Merlin had explained them. A great throne-chair, with a crown carved at the top of the high back, was placed at the upper end, just under the eastern window, blazoned with the finding of Excalibur; and all around the table stood the chairs of the knights, with the crest and shield of each carved at the back. Opposite the king's chair stood another, wrought with many magic arts by Merlin, and named by him the Siege (or seat) Perilous, for, as he had warned the knights, no man might sit in it except the one for whom it was intended; and if any other should venture, some great peril was sure to befall him.

 But soon after this chair was placed, and in spite of his own warning, Merlin had by some evil charge seated himself in it, and had immediately disappeared, whither no one knew, although all still looked for his return. Since then, Sir Galahad, feeling himself called to a high and noble effort of chivalry, had dared to place himself in the Siege Perilous. Seated therein, he had seen the vision of the Holy Grail for which he was about to seek, and found himself mightily

strengthened and encouraged thereby. After that he
departed upon his quest, and followed it to the end.
Having seen the Holy Grail, he departed from earth, and
crossing the seas in the moonglade, came straight to the
land where he and his comrades now dwell forever ; and
whither Arthur, after that last great battle in the west,
had been brought by those three queens who loved him,
Morgana le Fay, Belisante his sister, and the mysterious
Lady of the Lake.

Since then no more had dared to sit in the Siege Per
ilous. So it stood empty, the only gap in the bright
circle of the knights, when Arthur and his chivalry
seated themselves about the Round Table for council, or
for friendly talk, or for the telling and hearing of knightly
deeds.

CHAPTER XV.

HOP-O'-MY-THUMB.

THE knights and ladies were all seated at the tables,
with the king and queen at the head of the centre
one, and the feast went on with mirth, and song, and
laughter.   Taliessin the bard was there, seated in a
place of honor, he struck his harp right joyously.   He
sang a song of love, of ladies' smiles, of feasting, and
the pouring of wine.   At the end of every verse, knights
and ladies smilingly joined in the chorus, sending great
floods of melody rolling up into the arched roof and out
through the twelve great windows, until the husband-
men binding sheaves in the yellow fields beside the

river paused in their happy labor, and raising their heads, said:

"There is feasting in our good king's hall to-day, and right merry are the noble knights, as well they may be, living in Arthur's presence."

Little Rhoda, looking and listening to everything, forgot to eat, except when her companion Sir Percivale urged some dainty morsel upon her, or laughed at her bewilderment. Sometimes at these moments she found the queen or Lady Isolde looking at her with scornful smiles, or frowns; and then she turned to the king's face, and in its grand sweetness and protecting power she found strength and comfort.

The feast was at its height when the great doors at the lower end of the hall were thrown open, and the chamberlain who waited just within them stepped forward, glanced at the new arrival, bowed lowly, and announced:

"The noble knight Sir Lancelot du Lac!"

A murmur of pleased surprise ran through the hall, and every eye was turned upon the doorway, through which appeared first Sir Lancelot, his armor soiled, cut, and disordered, his head bare, his face pale and worn, but his bearing upright and fearless as it had right to be. Behind him followed a giant, whose great head was bowed in entering the lofty doorway, and who carried upon his shoulder a dwarf hardly three feet in height, with a face so wrinkled and so droll that no one could look upon it without laughter. The giant was disarmed and his hands were loosely tied by one end of a long rope, the other end of which was bound tightly around the arms of a knight, in whom Rhoda recognized with a shudder Sir Guy du Fontaine.

Followed by these his captives, Sir Lancelot strode up the hall until, reaching the head of the centre table, he stopped, and addressing the king, said:

"I have, first of all, my Lord Arthur, to crave pardon for appearing thus before your majesty; but mine errand must be my excuse, for I bring you first a false and forsworn knight, whom but this morning I conquered fairly, and who with my dagger at his throat yielded himself my prisoner, passing his word, as knight and gentleman, to practise nothing farther against me or a certain lady whom I had the good fortune to rescue from his hands. After that, losing my horse, I was making my way through the wood on foot, when I again encountered mine enemy, who seeing me dismounted and partially disarmed, set upon me with murderous intent; and but that God and my Lady helped me, he had slain me. But in the end I conquered once again, so wounding him that I think he will be content to rest awhile from his evil deeds. Then mounting my captive's horse, and leading him, pinioned as you see him, I rode softly on until at a turn of the road I came upon this giant carrying the dwarf. He was driving before him a herd of beeves, of which he had robbed a luckless hind, taking him captive also. Perceiving me, the herdsman ran forward in spite of the giant's threats, and kneeling, set forth his hard case, begging for help and redress.

"The story told, I ordered the giant to give up his ill-gotten booty and release his prisoner, the which demands he refused with insolence, and swinging his iron mace about his head, dared me to attack him. This was not to be endured, and making suddenly in, I struck him so shrewd a blow upon the sword-arm that the mace fell crashing to the ground, and well-nigh the arm with it. A few more blows brought my poor giant to his knees and to reason; whereupon I bound up his arm, tied him to the other end of the rope already securing

my first captive, and so brought him forward, thinking that my Lord Arthur might accept the giant, and my liege lady the queen might fancy the dwarf, as humble offerings from their unworthy knight Lancelot."

"Many thanks, fair knight and brother; and we accept the gift right joyously," replied the king graciously. "And what of your other captive, Sir Guy du Fontaine?"

"He also is at Your Grace's disposal, for I can make no terms, even those of honorable enmity, with a dastard and a liar."

"Nor can we count such among the knighthood of our realm," replied the king gravely. "We have already heard of Sir Guy du Fontaine's misdeeds from the Lady Isolde of Escourt. We now ordain that he be for to-night kept in close ward, and that to-morrow, before the jousts begin, he shall stand upon a scaffold in face of all the court; and that then and there his spurs shall be hacked from his heels by the common headsman, the crest shall be shorn from his helmet, and the bearings upon his shield shall be effaced and blotted from our roll of armorial and knightly bearings. So let it be."

A great silence fell upon the hall as this severe and terrible sentence passed from the lips of the good king, who never blamed without cause, or punished when he could forgive. Even Guy du Fontaine bowed his head without a word; and when the king's guards approached to unbind and lead him away, he followed without resistance.

"Heaven be praised that he was never of the Round Table," said Sir Percivale, looking sternly after the dishonored knight.

"I suppose the king knew that none of those he chose for the Round Table could do anything mean or wicked," said Rhoda.

"Think you so, little maid?" asked her companion smiling brightly. "However that may have been, full well do all of us feel, that being chosen, we no longer belong to the world or to ourselves, but to our lord the king, and through him to his Lord, who is the Lord of heaven and earth."

As he said these words, Sir Percivale's face glowed with a joy at once so sweet and so solemn, that Rhoda looked at him without daring to reply; and in the pause Sir Lancelot's voice was heard:

"And now, if my lord the king excuses me, I will go and lay off this stained and cumbrous armor, and don garments better suited to ladies' presence and royal feasting."

"Go, but return anon, fair sir," replied the king; and the queen coldly added:

"And prithee, Sir Lancelot, take the giant and the dwarf away with you. They spoil our merriment with their ugliness."

"I had hoped that your majesty would accept the dwarf as an offering from the humblest of your knights," replied Sir Lancelot, bowing lowly, and suffering his eyes to rest reproachfully upon the queen's haughty face. But she shook her head disdainfully, and waving her hand, said:

"Nay, I care not for such grewsome playthings, give him rather to the little lady of the wood who came hither riding your war-horse, and with her mouth full of the praises of Sir Lancelot du Lac. There she sits beside Sir Percivale, who is, I fear, your too successful rival in her good graces."

"Your majesty shall be obeyed," replied Sir Lancelot again bowing almost to the ground; but as he raised his head, those who watched him saw the angry flush which not all his pride could control. Then, signing to the dwarf to follow him, he passed on to where Rhoda was sitting, and said:

"Pardon me, fair lady, that I have not before offered you my respectful thanks for your kind company in the wood, and your gentle patience when I was forced to leave you for a time. Will you kindly accept from me this dwarf, who, little though he be, is so quick of wit and limb that he cannot fail to become a valuable servant, and may at least serve to remind you sometimes of Lancelot."

"Very prettily spoken; but in fact all the world knows that Sir Lancelot du Lac is always ready with pretty speeches for every child or woman who will listen to him," said the queen, laughing scornfully. Guinevere the Fair could not endure that those she liked should offer even courtesy to any other than herself; and being queen and almost undisputed in whatever she said or did, she had never learned to hide or restrain her jealous temper. But Lancelot never looked toward her or seemed to listen to her biting words, as he stood bending over Rhoda's chair, waiting for the answer which she did not know how to make.

At this moment a slight disturbance was heard at the door, and a woman pressing her way through the guards came forward, followed timidly by a man dressed as a common laborer, and appearing much confused at finding himself in such a place and company.

"I must see the king! I must speak to our good Lord Arthur; he will see me righted; he is father of all his people!" cried the woman.

Arthur, turning toward her, said: "Let her approach. What would you of the king, dame?"

"Justice, Lord Arthur. That dwarf is my child, my poor little Hop-o'-my-thumb, and he was stolen away from me only this morning by Grogoram the Giant, who surprised him playing in our field beside the river; and who took him and our two poor cows, with all our neighbor's cattle, while we ran up and down, not knowing where to look for child or kine. Edmund our neighbor came creeping home well-nigh dead with fright and weariness, and told us how a brave knight of the king's court had taken the giant prisoner, and with him our poor little manikin here; and how he would carry them as gifts to the king and queen. Now, O Lord Arthur, how can any man make gift of a child whose mother claims him, and holds out her arms to him, and calls him—so!"

And the poor woman, throwing herself upon her knees, raised her face streaming with tears toward the king, and stretched her arms toward the dwarf, whose wrinkled face began to work, and his little body to tremble all over with eagerness, although he stood patient and silent beside his master, Sir Lancelot. Looking kindly toward him, Arthur held out his hand.

"Come hither, manikin. Is the good woman's story true, and she really thy mother?"

"Yes, my Lord King, and a right good mother too," replied Hop-o'-my-thumb, kneeling beside the king's chair, and speaking in a strange high-pitched voice.

"And you would like to return home with her, rather than to take service here at court, or wherever Sir Lancelot, your captor, might appoint?"

"Yes, your majesty. In my father's cabin I call no one master, unless it be my mother; but in service, a little fellow like me must be every man's servant.

"You speak shrewdly as well as drolly, manikin," replied the king, smiling. "And if Sir Lancelot du Lac consents to release his claim, thou art free to follow thy mother-master this very instant. How is it, Sir Lancelot?"

"My claims upon the dwarf are already bestowed in this lady's hands, your majesty," replied the knight, bowing gravely.

"And you, fair maid? Will you return him to his mother, and his home?" asked the king.

"Oh, yes. I did not want him, any way," began Rhoda hastily; and then fearing to be rude, added hesitatingly, "Though I was very much obliged to you, sir, for giving him to me."

"My poor gifts seem unfortunate to-day, but it is as well," replied Lancelot, looking at the queen, who would have spoken; but the king was already saying to his attendant:

"Let a handful of broad pieces be given to the dwarf, and see him safely beyond the town; and you, my Lancelot, go get thee ready for at least the end of the feast, and return right speedily."

Bowing reverently, but without other reply, Lancelot withdrew from the royal presence, and though the revel lasted far into the night, he did not appear again, either at the feast or the dance which followed it.

CHAPTER XVI.

THE TOURNAMENT.

THE day following that of Rhoda's arrival at Camelot was appointed for a grand tournament or joust,
when all the knights of Arthur's court, and as many
besides as chose to attend, were to tilt with blunted lances
and edgeless swords, fighting not for life, but glory and
ladies' smiles.

The lists were set in a beautiful green meadow beside
the river Usk, and at an early hour the whole court set
forth, the knights riding their war-chargers; and the
ladies their palfreys or jennets, all dressed in their best
array, and wearing their gayest faces.

Rhoda, mounted upon a pretty pony, rode between
the Lady Isolde and another lady of the court, who had

been desired to take charge of her, but who was too busy chatting with the gay young squire beside her to pay much attention to her young companion, while the Lady Isolde never looked toward her.

Rhoda, thus left to herself, glanced curiously about her, examining everything and wondering at everything. Reaching the top of a little hill just outside the town, she saw in the wide meadow at its foot a space of ground closed in at the ends by stout and high barriers, and at the sides by galleries with benches beneath, for the use of the spectators fortunate enough to find room upon them.

In the centre of each of these rows of galleries was one higher and more ornamented than the rest. Over that at the right hand was a golden crown, and above it floated the dragon banner, marking it for the royal seat. Over the other was also suspended a crown, but this was only of tinsel and flowers, and a banner representing Cupid surrounded by roses: this gallery was intended for the Queen of Love and Beauty, to be chosen by the knight most successful in the first melée, as the general combat was called in distinction to those single combats where only two knights contended. Outside the barriers at the ends of the lists were pitched several pavilions and tents for the use of the knights, and at the doors of these tents were already planted the banners of many of Arthur's best-known lances, while their squires and pages, hurrying in and out, polishing anew some piece of armor already dazzlingly bright, or holding their masters' splendid war-horses ready for mounting, gave life and action to the scene.

Rhoda was led by her companion to seats reserved for them in one of the principal galleries, and, as soon as she was placed, began to search among the banners for that of her friend Lancelot, which displayed upon a silver ground a knight in full armor, with the red cross of a crusader upon his shoulder, kneeling at a lady's feet.

"There he is!" cried she joyfully, as she discovered this device floating out from amidst several others, before one of the principal tents.

"There is who?" asked Lady Isolde sharply.

"Sir Lancelot; and yes, that is Sir Percivale's pennon beside it, and Sir Galahad's too. The three have that tent together; isn't it nice?"

"It seems to me, young mistress, that you have learned to talk very glibly of the names and devices of knights, not one of whom you ever saw until yesterday, I think."

"They have been very kind to me; and Sir Percirale told me all about the banners last night, and told me to look for his; and he said he would wear a rose on his helmet for me to know him, and—"

But here Rhoda stopped, almost frightened at the scornful and angry look cast upon her by Isolde, while the lady at her other side laughed aloud, saying:

"She leaves us all behind, does she not, Lady Isolde? Lancelot sets her upon his own steed, and Percivale wears her favor at a solemn festival and joust. Hath not our Lord Arthur also given thee some token of his regard, fair Mistress Rhoda?"

"No, ma'am, except being very kind to me; and I suppose that was because I am all alone here, and do not know how to take care of myself as the rest of you do," said Rhoda gravely; and the lady, still laughing, cried:

"My faith, but the little thing is giving us lessons in courtesy and hospitality. Gramercy, my Lady Isolde, we shall do well to look to our words in such fine company—"

But the sentence was cut short by a loud and long flourish of trumpets, announcing that the lists were opened, and the joust about to begin, and at once all eyes and ears and thoughts were turned toward the barriers, behind which the knights were now seen ranged in two long bright lines, armor glittering, pennons waving, lances in rest, and chargers fretting and pawing in their eagerness for the fray.

Out from their small and gayly decorated tents now

stepped the heralds, one at either end of the lists, and in the stately jargon, of their calling, first one and then the other announced the names and titles of the knights about to enter from his end of the lists, adding a hope for their success, and that God would prosper the right.

Then, at a signal from the heralds, the barriers were thrown down, the trumpets sounded the onset, and the two long glittering lines of knights moved rapidly forward, breaking, as they entered the lists, into a sharp gallop, increasing in speed until about the centre of the lists they met, with a loud clash of spears rattling upon shield or armor, a din of war-cries, the shrill neighing of horses, and the loud cries of the spectators, who shouted the name of this or that favorite knight, encouraging him on to victory.

Before this first great shock of onset more than half of all the knights went down, either driven backward from their saddles, or overthrown, horse and man together, and rolled helpless beneath the feet of those still saddle-fast. By the rules of the tournament, every knight thus overthrown was judged defeated, and was obliged to withdraw at once from the lists, although he might enter himself again for any other encounter. These unlucky ones were now seen struggling to their feet, some unharmed, but most of them bruised and shaken, and a few so injured as to be unable to rise without the help of their squires, who made in to their masters' rescue as fast as possible, and not without some danger to themselves. These and the riderless horses removed, the lists were cleared for another course, the knights withdrawing as far as the barriers, and charging down upon each other as before, with like results, except that now the lists being less crowded, the knights were able to select their opponents, and after the first encounter with the lance, to continue the struggle with the sword either on foot or horseback. Whenever a knight was overthrown, or beaten to his knee, or driven back until he touched the barriers, he was judged defeated, and forced to withdraw.

After a little time the lists were almost deserted except by Lancelot, Galahad, Percivale, and a few knights, who, having conquered all others, felt eager to match themselves against these, the three champions of Arthur's court.

In the next course three more were defeated, and while Sir Lancelot ran a course with his cousin, the brave Sir Bors, the other two separated for a friendly trial of strength against each other. Two more upon each side opposed themselves, and at the signal the whole eight met with a clash and a shock that sent three of the nameless knights and the gallant Sir Bors reeling to the ground, while Sir Galahad and Sir Percivale, splintering their lances fairly in the centre of each other's shield, rode on to the farther end of the lists and passed out, neither claiming the victory. The solitary knight who retained his saddle cared not to risk his laurels by riding against Sir Lancelot, and, saluting him as victor, left the field, amid the cheers of his especial friends, who held him as all but conqueror, since no man ever hoped to quite equal Lancelot.

And now, with a joyous flourish of trumpets and wild cries of joy and admiration from the crowd, the heralds proclaimed Sir Lancelot du Lac victor of the day, and master of the lists. To him was delivered the pretty crown of filagree gold, which was at once his prize and the offering he was to lay at the feet of the lady whom he might choose as Queen of Love and Beauty.

Receiving this crown upon the point of his lance, and baring his handsome head, Sir Lancelot, restraining his horse to a walk, passed around the lists close beneath the galleries, looking up with merry and admiring glances at the long lines of beautiful, eager faces bending over to watch his progress.

Reaching the royal gallery, he checked Tonnerre still more, and fixing his glance upon the queen's face, was about to lower the lance and lay his trophy at her feet; but Guinevere, still vexed and pettish because he had remained away from the feast and dance, now glanced slightly at him, and turning away, feigned to be so busy in whispering some laughing words in the king's ear that she could not see the knight, who hesitated for a moment, waiting to catch her eye. No longer able to doubt that she intended to slight him and his offering, Lancelot raised his head proudly erect, recovered his drooping lance, and rode on, bowing profoundly as he passed the king, but never looking again at the haughty queen, whose rich color faded, and whose blue eyes sparkled with anger, although she still feigned to be too busy to look toward him.

" Do you see that, Lady Ermengarde?" eagerly murmured Isolde, leaning across Rhoda to speak to her companion. " The queen slights Lancelot before all the court, and some of us poor mortals must be his choice, and wear the crown. See, here he comes!"

And both ladies bent their eyes upon Lancelot, who, no longer careless and gay, but with a fixed and scornful smile upon his lips, rode on, fretting his horse with the spur, and at the same time checking him with the curb, so that he bounded, curvetted, and caracoled in a manner that would have made it difficult for a less experienced rider to retain his seat.

Lancelot, hardly seeming to remember that he was upon horseback, carelessly allowed his eyes to roam over the crowded benches. Meeting the Lady Isolde's pointed regard and smile, he bowed, and then his eyes passing on to Rhoda's eager little face, a gentler look came over his own, and suddenly lowering his lance he laid the crown upon her lap, bowing at the same

time until his coal-black curls mingled with Tonnerre's
mane.

A pause of utter surprise and doubt held every
tongue and eye fixed for a moment, while Rhoda sat,
the crown upon her folded hands, her eyes fixed upon
Sir Lancelot; the Lady Isolde's face grew dark with
envy and vexation, and the Lady Ermengarde stared as
if unable to credit her own eyes. Lancelot was the first
to speak:

"Fair maiden, will you accept my prize, and with it
crown yourself Queen of Love and Beauty?" asked he;
and Rhoda, her courage and her wits flowing back to
her, raised the crown from her lap, and said in her soft
childish voice:

"Thank you, Sir Lancelot; but it is only because
you are so kind that you give it to me. I am not—"

"Prythee hush, Miss Malapert!" whispered Ermengarde in her ear. "You are not to judge the wisdom
of the good knight's choice, but accept it gratefully.
Put the crown upon thy foolish head, and bow and smile."

Without reply Rhoda obeyed, the trumpets rang out
a salute, the heralds announced her name and her title.
Noon had now arrived, the knights retired to their tents,
the royal party to a pavilion prepared for them, the
better sort of spectators to shaded spots beside the river,
or to private tents, while the common people, drawing
their luncheon from their wallets or baskets, picnicked in
the shade of the galleries where they sat.

Rhoda, invited by a special messenger, was led to the royal pavilion, where, seated beside Sir Lancelot, she received the smiles and attention due to the Queen of Love and Beauty and the chosen lady of Arthur's mightiest knight.

CHAPTER XVII.

THE MANTLE AND THE DRINKING-HORN.

BESIDES Rhoda and Sir Lancelot, the king and
queen had invited many other guests to the luncheon served in their pavilion. The feasting and merriment were at their highest when a chamberlain glided
into the tent, and passing behind the king's chair, whispered something in his ear. Arthur smiled, and raising
his hand for silence, said aloud:

"Knights and ladies, one waits without with two
rare and precious commodities, which he will bestow
upon any among us who may deserve them. Give
your attention then, for I have sent for him to enter."

The buzz of words and laughter ceased upon the
moment, and every face was turned toward the door of

the tent, where now appeared a boy perhaps twelve years old, with a laughing yet overwise expression upon his handsome face, and a basket upon his arm. Holding his gay cap in his hand, he passed quickly through the tent until, reaching the head of the table, he knelt beside the king's chair, and humbly bowed his head. Looking kindly at him, Arthur said :

" Well, child, what is it you have there ? "

" A mantle and a drinking-horn, fair king," replied the boy. " A mantle that will lend beauty and grace to whoever wears it, so that she remain true and pure, and a horn from which a brave man may always drink without refilling, so long as he remains brave. But, O king, the wonder still remains to be told, for, such are the magic virtues of mantle and horn, that no woman who has ever told a lie, or even acted one, can wear the mantle; and no man who has ever shown himself coward or traitor can drink from the horn ; and these rich possessions are now mine own, and shall belong to her and to him who can prove their right to possess them, if such lady and knight can be found in this goodly company."

" And what, that either knight or lady can offer, will repay you for such rich and curious gifts, fair son ? " asked the king, smiling good-humoredly.

" A kiss upon my mouth from the lady, and some help against mine enemies from the knight," replied the boy boldly. At the answer all the ladies smiled and looked at each other, some angrily, some bashfully, or archly, while the knights laughed aloud, and one said, "The mantle would seem to be of far greater value than the horn, since the price is so much heavier. Would it not be well, brothers, that we all turn venders of mantles?"

Without heeding words or looks, the boy set his basket upon the ground, and drew from it first a cloak or mantle of purple silk, curiously and richly embroidered with gold thread, with a sentence wrought around the hem in a language which none of all the court could read. It had a great golden clasp, set with a changing moonstone, to fasten it about the throat, and it was altogether so rich and beautiful a garment that any lady might have been proud to wear it, apart from its magic qualities.

Shaking out its rustling folds, and moving it this way and that, the boy held it up to the light, and turning toward Guinevere's chair of state, he said:

"Will the queen deign to try my poor mantle?"

"What, and give thee a kiss for it, malapert! The request is something over-bold," replied Guinevere haughtily, and the king added more gently:

"Our queen's truth needs no proving, nor could she bestow the priceless gift you ask, fair child; but these her ladies, all true and good, as who shall doubt, may well amuse themselves with the sport you bring them. What say you, Lady Ermengarde? May the boy lay his pretty mantle upon your shoulders?"

"At your majesty's command," replied Ermengarde

humbly, yet not with any great willingness; and rising
she approached the youth, who, smiling in his subtle
fashion, threw the cloak across her shoulders; but no
sooner had it rested there, than with a crackling, rending
noise it split in twenty places from top to bottom, each
strip curling and writhing like a serpent, so that the lady,
screaming loudly, threw it from her, crying, "It is alive!
it stings! it chokes me!"

> "My cloak is but of silk and gold,
>   And cannot sting, fair dame;
>   It is the falsehoods you have told
>   That bring you now to shame!"

said the boy quietly, taking the mantle from the ground,
shaking it, and showing it whole and perfect as before.

"There is a trick about it. The varlet has contrived
this trick to put us all to shame!" exclaimed Vivien
passionately. "Here, boy, give it me in mine own hands,
and let me see if I can not wear it without such mis-
chance."

Without reply the boy held out the mantle, and the
lady, one of the most beautiful and least beloved of the
whole court, took it, and carrying it to a little distance
from him, threw it lightly about her; but at that very
instant the mantle broke or seemed to break into a sudden flame, and blazing upward, surrounded Vivien's head
with fire, so that, shrieking and stamping, she tore the
cloak from her shoulders, while every one rose in con-

fusion and ran to help her; but the boy, snatching it from the ground, sang loudly:

> " Lady, that fire was but a sign
>   Of fires that hotter, fiercer barn ;
>   They do not come from me or mine,
>   But shall be yours, unless you turn."

"What! is there never a lady here that can wear this scandalous cloak in safety?" cried Sir Craddocke, a grim, gray-haired knight, sitting beside his wife, toward whom he turned, and added:

"Get thee forward, dame, and put the thing about thee! These ten years that thou hast been my wife I have proved thee true and leal, and if the mantle shames thee, I for one shall know it for a lying mantle, and its malapert owner for a knave that needs a beating."

Modestly, yet without fear, the lady stepped forward, and Sir Craddocke himself laid the mantle across her shoulders. For a moment it hung there straight and whole, and the husband cried triumphantly:

"See! Here is one true dame, if no more—"

But the boy with his strange and mocking smile laid a hand upon Sir Craddocke's arm, and pointed downward to where the hem of the mantle was beginning to shrink and crack and draw upward as if withered and decayed.

"It is the falsehood I passed upon my father and mother, when I stole away from them and home to marry you, Sir Craddocke," sobbed the lady, and covering her crimson face with her hands she began to cry; but her husband, snatching the mantle from her shoulders, folded his arms about her, and kissing her before the whole court, he exclaimed:

" Well, then, Dame Kate, since that is thine only falsehood, and that was acted for love of me, it is not for me to chide thee or value thee the less for it; so come and sit thee down again, and watch the play out."

But as Sir Craddocke tenderly led his dame back to her seat, the boy, shaking and turning the mantle, sang:

> " Who cheats her father and her mother,
> Even for true love's sake,
> May cheat her lover for another,
> And holiest vows may break."

The fiery knight did not hear the warning, which would certainly have made him angry; and Sir Percivale, kindly wishing to turn the attention of the whispering crowd from Dame Kate, rose, and taking the mantle from the boy, brought the mantle to Rhoda, saying:

" Dear little Rose, you will not refuse to allow me to put the mantle about you; for surely one so young, and wearing such a look of truth and purity, can have done no wrong."

But Rhoda, springing from her chair, stepped backward in alarm, crying:

" No, no! Don't put it on me. I have told wrong

stories ever so many times when I was little, and I am afraid!"

"But none since you were old enough to know right from wrong, surely?" asked the knight gravely.

N---o, sir—that is, I don't remember any," said Rhoda faintly. "But I'm afraid those will count."

"Oh, no, they were but childish errors, and are past," persisted Sir Percivale, throwing the cloak about her; but before it touched her shoulders, the boy snatched it and replaced it in his basket, singing as he did so:

"Childish falsehoods may stain the child,
But pass when she is older grown:
Maid, if you live true, pure, and mild,
The mantle yet shall be your own."

Then, without waiting for further question or remark, he took from the basket a curiously wrought drinking-horn of ivory, inlaid with silver, and supported upon three feet of the same metal. This the boy filled with wine from one of the great flagons upon the table, and holding it toward the king, said:

"Here is what shall show, O king, the true courage and temper of these your knights and courtiers; for never coward or traitor can drink from it, let him try his best."

"Say you so?" cried the king pleasantly. "Ther shall you, my Lancelot, drink from it first; for all men know you as the flower of knighthood, and bravest, even where all are brave and true. Drink, fair sir, to my Dame Guinevere, and to me also, if so it please you."

Lancelot took the cup, and turning his dark and troubled face first to one and then the other, he muttered hoarsely: "I drink to my king and to his queen," and raised the cup to his lips; but whether it was that his hand shook, or that the cup was over-full, or that the boy had so contrived it, before it reached his lips it turned, and all the wine was spilled upon the ground. A sort of horror fell upon the court, and even the king looked aghast, while Lancelot, never moving or speaking, stood with the empty drinking-horn in his hand, and his eyes moodily downcast, while the boy chanted mockingly:

"Behold the knight who never played a coward's part,
But yet is traitor in his inmost heart!"

"My Lancelot a traitor!" cried Arthur indignantly. "Nay, boy, now thou dost indeed exceed thy license; and well can we all see that thou art but a juggling rascal. Lancelot du Lac coward or traitor! Never, while the sun shines, or the seas roll, or thou, Guinevere, art fair and true! Here, give me the horn, for I do believe that it is so fashioned that no man may drink from it. Let not the boy touch it, but, Lancelot, do thou fill and bear it to me."

Without reply the knight obeyed, filled the cup again from the same flagon, and, still with his eyes fixed moodily upon the floor, carried it and gave it to the king, who taking it, slowly turned his blue eyes from one to another of his knights, saying :

"I drink first to Lancelot du Lac, and after him to all brave men and true."

Then he raised the cup to his lips, drank off the wine without a pause, and held out the empty and reversed cup, that all might see that it was emptied.

"The spell is broken, knights and gentlemen," said he gayly; "and any now may use the drinking-horn, so that he does not let its owner meddle with it."

> "Our lord the king is leal and true,
>   As who shall dare to doubt?
> If there's one like him 'mong you,
>   The horn will soon find out,"

sang the boy; and when at a sign from the king the chamberlain filled the horn and offered it to one and another, so many hung back, or turned away, or showed in various ways that they did not wish for the test, that the king, his face pale and shocked, hastily cried :

"Away with this folly! My knights need no magic to prove them brave and true. Return the cup to the boy; and hark, the heralds summon us to the lists. My queen, will you break up the banquet?"

And as the company rose in some confusion, the boy, with the mantle and the cup still in his possession, passed from the tent and was seen no more.

CHAPTER XVIII.

FAIRY SPECTACLES.

AS Rhoda, following the king and queen, returned to the lists, she was met by the heralds, who in solemn and almost unintelligible language told her that, as Queen of Love and Beauty, her place was now in the gallery opposite that of the king and queen, and that they were ready to escort her thither.

Half pleased, and half frightened, Rhoda followed them, and took her place beneath the canopy. Then Sir Lancelot, who had been also summoned, placed the crown upon her head, and kneeling, kissed her hand in token of homage to her royal station. Then he and the heralds left the gallery, and she remained alone, the centre of a sea of eyes that seemed to her without limit.

And now the course was cleared, the barriers thrown down, and the heralds announced that the lists were open to any knights who, having exchanged challenges and given their names to the heralds, might choose to ride against each other with sharp spears and swords, the combat to be decided by the first blood drawn, or by either knight yielding himself vanquished. The first victor would receive as prize a silver lance-head bestowed upon him by the Queen of Love and Beauty; the second would have a sword-hilt; the third a pair of spurs; and the fourth a silken scarf. Each victor should have the privilege of challenging any knight who had not yet ridden; but those once vanquished were not permit ted to enter the lists again that afternoon, and the prizes were not to be awarded until the jousts were ended for the day.

These terms announced, the trumpets sounded a fanciful flourish, and in at each end of the lists rode six knights; the one party, called the challenged, re-mained stationary just inside the barriers, while the other, called the challengers, rode rapidly forward, and each lightly touched with his spear-point the shield of him whom he wished to oppose. These ranged them-selves opposite to their challengers, who, wheeling their horses, returned to their own end of the lists, wheeled again, and at the sound of the trumpets both bands gal-loped forward, meeting midway with a tremendous shock. Five knights and three horses went down, and when the squires hastened to their masters' rescue it was discovered that Sir Wulstan lay dead in his harness, with a spear-head in his brain; that the Knight of Wynn had a leg crushed beneath his dead horse; and that another, calling himself The Unknown, was so bruised and shaken by his fall as to be unable to stand or speak. The other two knights, confessing themselves conquered, slowly left the field, their horses and armor becoming the prize of the victors, unless the latter courteously consented to remit the penalty, or to accept a sum of money in place of it. The knights who remained, dismounted, and drawing their swords, continued the combat on foot, some of them, however, gayly and courteously, as a mere passage of arms. One pair at least fought with the eager fury of real anger, and dealt blows so hard and so keen that before many moments both were wounded, and one at least might have been killed outright, but that the heralds interfered to remind the knights that by the laws of the field every combat ended with the first blood drawn, and that private quarrels of a deadly nature were not to be allowed in lists only intended for a fair and gentle passage at arms.

It was at this moment, while Rhoda was watching with mingled terror and admiration the two knights who fought beneath her balcony, that a voice whispered in her ear:

"The carriage is waiting; and I should think you had had enough of this fools' play."

13

Turning with a start, Rhoda joyfully recognized the Chimney-Elf perched cross-legged upon the back of her chair, his pointed cap hanging jauntily over one eye, and a long pipe in his mouth, from which he drew such clouds of smoke as almost to hide himself from sight.

"Oh, Chimney-Elf, is it you?" cried Rhoda, "Why did you run away from me, and where have you been, and how did you find me out?"

"Just your old way!" muttered the elf peevishly. "Three questions in a breath; and I won't answer one of them. It is enough for you to know that I am here, and want you to come home."

"Home?" repeated Rhoda dreamily, for she had begun to feel as if what Sir Percivale had told her was true—that this was the real life, and what she had known before, was only a dream already half forgotten.

"Yes, home; and here is the fairy godmother kindly come to take you part way; why don't you speak to her?" asked the Chimney-Elf impatiently. Rhoda suddenly became aware that the chariot and griffins were standing beside her, and that the fairy godmother, holding the whip and reins in one hand, was reaching the other toward her, saying impatiently:

"Come, little girl, step in as quickly as you can! The griffins won't stand, and I am in a hurry," while the Chimney-Elf added in the same tone:

"Come, Rhoda, jump in, and don't dawdle."

"But the tournament!—but Sir Percivale, and Sir

Lancelot, and the prizes; and I am the Queen of Love and Beauty, and am to give them away!" cried Rhoda in dismay; but even as she spoke she yielded, and stepped into the chariot, which was instantly whirled up into the air; and in another moment, Camelot, and the bright Usk, and the lists, and the whole gay scene of which but now Rhoda had formed a part, mingled together in one glittering, restless mass, then grew vague and indistinct, and at last was hidden beneath the low clouds scudding between the chariot and the moon's surface. The Chimney-Elf wrapped himself closely and sullenly in a great gray mantle, or perhaps it was nothing but a smoke-wreath somewhat denser than common; the fairy gave all her attention to the griffins; Rhoda, with her eyes full of tears and her head bent upon her hand, was musing over the scenes she had just left, wondering if she never again should see the friends she had already learnt to love, when the chariot touched the ground with a shock that at once aroused her. Raising her dim eyes, she saw that they had reached the sea-shore, and that at the head of the wide gold-sanded beach stood a building whose many windows, tall chimneys, and whirling noises reminded the little girl of the factory buildings she had once been to visit in Lowell. The fairy's first words confirmed the idea:

"I have to go in here to order a quantity of glasses for his Majesty of Lilliput," said she. "After that I will take you round by the cloud-palaces, and so to the

Moonglade beach, where you will find your boat. Do you want to come in, Rhoda?"

"Yes, if you please, ma'am; but what sort of a place is it?" asked the little girl, privately thinking that it was a very poor exchange for her dear Camelot. The fairy glanced at her shrewdly, and replied:

"No, it isn't as romantic, but it's more to the purpose, I assure you. This is my spectacle factory. Come along."

"I shouldn't think you would need spectacles, ma'am," said Rhoda, feeling that it was as well to speak out her thoughts as to have them read in this manner.

"Why not?"

"I thought fairies could do all they wanted to, and see and hear everything ever so far off, and—"

"All true my dear, and I do not need the spectacles for myself. I manufacture them for the market."

"Oh! do you, ma'am?" stammered Rhoda, more and more bewildered.

"Yes," returned the fairy godmother complacently "I sell a great many spectacles, both here, and down below in your world. Our principal trade, however, is with Lilliput. The glasses magnify, you see, and the Lilliputians, when they get them on, feel themselves equal to anybody. They also have the faculty of making everything seen through them look just as the person looking wishes to see it. We sell great numbers to fond mammas, who look at their children through them; also to aged husbands of young wives; also to foolish wives of wicked husbands; and as for lovers, both male and female, they always provide themselves with fairy spectacles before they buy the engagement ring."

"But how do all these people find you out, and how do they pay you for the spectacles?" asked Rhoda.

"They don't find me out; they don't even know when they buy their glasses," replied the fairy, laughing maliciously. "I see that they need them, and I just fit on a pair and take my pay, without the other party being a bit the wiser."

"But what pay?"

"Well, it varies; but it is mostly in common sense. We fairies need a great deal of sense to manage all the affairs we have to handle; and the sorts of people I have mentioned don't seem to have any use at all for it; so I just take the sense they don't use, and give them fairy spectacles instead; so both parties are suited, don't you see?"

"And how do the Lilliputians pay you? In sense, too?" asked Rhoda, laughing.

"No, in babies."

"In—babies!"

"Yes, we bring them up for fairies. We used to get them from the world, but now that the Shakers have taken to the same business, the supply runs short; so we buy Lilliput babies, and pay in spectacles. But there, I can't stop to talk any longer; stand just where you are until I come back."

So saying, the fairy godmother took a hasty pinch of rose-pollen snuff, and went clicking down the great hall in her red-heeled shoes, striking her staff upon the stone floor as she went, and casting quick, sharp glances about her upon every side. In this great hall stood at least a dozen furnaces, each one surrounded by a crowd of little swarthy gnomes, their faces streaming with perspiration, and their eyes blood-shot and bleared from staring at the blinding fires. Some of these gnomes worked a machine which fed the furnaces with coals, some of them shook the grates and urged up the fires, some of them skimmed the boiling caldrons of liquid glass, and some of them swung these caldrons off from the furnaces, and ladled it into the moulds where the spectacle glasses were formed. At the lower end of the hall were two great folding doors opening into another hall, where the glasses were ground, polished, and mounted, and made ready for sale.

Rhoda was still looking about her, full of interest in all she saw, when the fairy godmother came clicking up the stone alley between the furnaces, with the master workman, a funny little black-and-red fellow, about two feet in height, walking a step behind her, and listening to her last orders.

"Fifty gross of lovers' rose-tinted spectacles, and the same number of true-blue ones for those American politicians who are going to make over the world; the gold-tinted ones for the authors to use in estimating the worth of their manuscripts, and the magnifiers for Lilliput. You have them all noted down?"

" Yes, madam, everything."

" And don't forget the green ones for those jealous husbands and wives. Poor wretches, they have paid all their peace and comfort for them, and we mustn't disappoint them of their bargain."

" Yes, madam," bowed the master gnome, smiling respectfully; and with a little nod of farewell, the fairy godmother clicked on and out of the spectacle factory, followed by Rhoda. As soon as they were seated in the chariot once more, she timidly asked:

" Could you let me have a pair, ma'am?"

" A pair of my spectacles, do you mean?"

" Yes, ma'am."

" Why, bless you child, you have worn them all your life. How else could you have seen the Chimney-Elf and his companions, and how could you have found the way to the moon, or even so much as seen me!"

" Was it all fairy spectacles, then?"

"Every bit of it. You have worn them nearly all your life, and I have fitted you with about five pair, of different sizes and qualities."

" And what have I given for them!" asked Rhoda, a little terrified, as she remembered the fairy's scornful remarks upon common sense; but the answer reassured her

"Not much that was worth keeping, my dear," said the fairy godmother, with a pleasant twinkle of her black eyes. "Only a little of your childish gayety, and content with common things, and a good deal of time and some little health. I believe that is about all. I am sure the spectacles have more than paid you. But it is about time for you to get some new ones. What do you say to a pair that will make the Widow Merriam, whom your father is to marry, look like a mother to you; and show you your sister Susy's lover, Jonas Merton, in a pleasanter light than you have seen him yet; and make your own home seem like a palace, or something better than a palace to you, and—"

"Oh, yes, yes, fairy godmother!" broke in Rhoda, with eyes flashing eagerly through their tears. "Those are the spectacles I want! Can you give them to me, and what can I give you instead?"

"They will cost you some of your self-will, some selfishness, some pride, and a good deal of trouble, my dear," replied the fairy kindly. "But I really think it will be an excellent bargain for you; and I have already fitted the glasses to your little nose, and will take my pay when I want it."

At this, Rhoda's hand went up to her nose, and the fairy added, laughing shrilly, "No, you can't feel them! Nobody knows whether they wear fairy spectacles or not; and it is one of the best jokes I know, to hear people praise their own clear-sightedness, and boast how far into a mill-stone it will carry them, when all the time, bless you, it is nothing but my glasses."

But Rhoda made no reply, for her mind was very full of thought, and the fairy godmother's laugh jarred upon her ear.

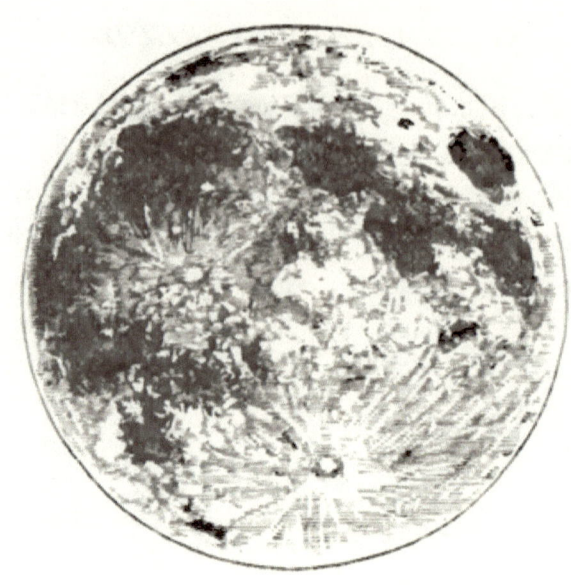

CHAPTER XIX.

DOWN THE MOONGLADE.

"WELL, Rhoda, are you going to keep me waiting much longer, I should like to know?" said the shrill voice of the Chimney-Elf. Rhoda, starting from her reverie, found herself standing upon the golden beach below the Man-in-the-Moon's house, with the dory drawn up at her feet, and her little friend already seated cross-legged upon the tiller and smoking furiously.

"Why! where is the fairy godmother, and the chariot, and the griffins?" exclaimed she, staring about her.

"Gone long ago, leaving you in such a stupid maze that you never knew when you got out, nor when I pulled down the dory, nor anything else. But here we are at one end of the moonglade, with home at the other. What do you say to starting?"

"Home!" echoed Rhoda drearily. "It seems so queer to think of home. And then it is so many years since I went away that they will have quite forgotten me. I don't believe I want to go home, Chimney-Elf."

"So many years!" repeated the elf with his shrillest laugh. "Well, well! Step into the boat, and when we reach home, if they do not know you, or if you do not want to stay, I will bring you back to the moon, and you may live here forever."

So Rhoda stepped into the dory, and took her seat in the bows as before, while the Chimney-Elf muttered some words which sent the little boat sliding down the sands and out upon the shining sea, already bright with the glories of the moonglade.

Presently Rhoda drooped her head, and hiding her face between her hands, she saw again the wondrous scenes through which she had so lately passed. She saw Sir Percivale's kindly eyes bent upon her as he placed her rose in his doublet; saw Sir Lancelot's stern beauty, and Arthur's kingly and gracious face; Guinevere's fair, false loveliness; and the jealous eyes of Isolde watching her as she sat at the feast beside Sir Percivale; and as she turned shuddering from that cruel gaze, the voice of the Chimney-Elf came drifting dreamily in upon her reverie:

"Get out, and go up to the house; your father has come home, and is asking for you."

"What! are we really at home, and is father here still!" murmured Rhoda, rubbing her eyes and looking about her. The dory lay beside the rude old wharf, as she had seen it so many times in the old days before her life in the moon; and she stepped out upon the mossy stones with a strange thrill of delight. It was like an old man's return to the home of his childhood. She looked about her, as he might do, with wonder that all should have remained so unchanged while she had lived so much and so long.

"I wonder who lives in the old house," murmured she at last; and slowly passing along the dewy moonlit path, she climbed the hill, and so through the grove and along the field, until, turning the corner of the gray old house, she met her father, who, patting her kindly upon the shoulder, said :

"Why, little girl, where have you been roaming? It is three or four hours since I first missed you, and it is growing late for little people to be about. When we have Mrs. Merriam here to look after things, she won't let you go on in this way."

"I have been out in the dory, father, but I am going right in, and to bed, now," said Rhoda aloud; while to herself she whispered, "I am afraid I shan't like it then so well as I do now; but I will always try to look at the

Widow Merriam through my fairy glasses. I wish I could be sure of always having them on."

"They will always be on when you wish for them, and, after a while, even without your wishing," whispered the Chimney-Elf, who, himself invisible, was riding home, very much at his ease, upon Rhoda's shoulder.

"Come, child!" exclaimed the father a little impatiently. "Don't stand dream-ing there; I want to shut the door. There, go right to bed, and to sleep. Good-night!"

"Good-night, father dear," replied the little girl, holding up her face for a kiss, and then, with a happy smile upon her lips, she passed into the dreamy old house, and up to her pretty bed-room, to live over in her dreams the fair scenes through which she had passed. While the Chimney-Elf, bounding from her shoulder to the hearth, and so up the chimney, curled himself to sleep in the sootiest corner, murmuring,

"Ah! there is no place like home, after all!"

Butler & Tanner, The Selwood Printing Works, Frome, and London.

www.ingramcontent.com/pod-product-compliance
Lightning Source LLC
Chambersburg PA
CBHW032007060726
47497CB00017B/2366